CODE PINK

A NOVEL

MARILYN METS

Code Pink

Copyright © 2023 Marilyn Baird Mets

Published by Seal Press

Paperback: 979-8-9883892-0-0
eISBN: 979-8-9883892-1-7

This is a work of fiction. References to real people, events, establishments, organizations, or locations are used fictitiously and are intended only to provide a sense of authenticity. All other names, characters, business, events and incidents are the products of the author's imagination. Any resemblance to actual persons, living or dead, or actual events is purely coincidental.

All Rights Reserved. No part of this book may be reproduced or transmitted in any form or by any means, electronic or mechanical, including photocopying, recording, or by any information retrieval or storage system, without the prior written consent of the publisher.

With love to my life-long partner,
LJM

And to our grandchildren,
Ainslie
Olivia
Ellinor
Abigail
and
Sam
The wish for full and fulfilling lives

CAST OF CHARACTERS

1840s and 1850s
    Eleanor Blakemore: first woman physician trained in the US; Joan's great-great-great-aunt

Joan's Household–1980 Chicago
    Joan Turner: third-year medical student
    Kathy Donaldson: Joan's roommate and classmate
    Erin Connelly: pediatric nurse who lives on the second floor of Joan's three-flat
    Rusty: Joan's Portuguese water dog
    Lily: Erin's poodle

Hospital Characters–1980 Chicago
    Jim Blakely: pediatrics resident
    Jay Peterson: ophthalmology resident
    Jackie Brown: nursery head nurse
    Ernie Smith: obstetrics and gynecology resident
    Peter Palmer: pathology resident
    Bill Baxter: cardiology resident
    Randy Olson: third-year medical student
    George Hull: third-year medical student

Joan's Family–1980 Medford, Massachusetts
- Liz Turner: Joan's mother
- Matt: Liz's boyfriend
- John Taylor: Joan's uncle and Liz's brother
- Anne Taylor: John's wife
- Adam Taylor: John and Anne's son and Joan's cousin

Patients–1980 Chicago
- Baby Boy Marsh: nursery patient
- Baby Girl White: nursery patient
- Baby Girl Jennings: nursery patient
- Denise Jennings: Baby Girl Jennings's mother
- Ricky: Denise's brother
- Seth Masters: diabetic patient
- Joey Miller: aniridia patient
- Scotty Green: shaken baby syndrome patient
- Baby Girl Murray: nursery patient
- Baby Boy Jones: nursery patient
- Baby Girl Patterson: nursery patient
- Sarah: obstetrics patient
- Anna: Sarah's newborn
- Jill: Sarah's sister
- Sasha: Jill's daughter
- Beverly Meadows: obstetrics patient
- Tom Meadows: Beverly's husband
- Baby Boy Bragg: nursery patient
- Shirley Bragg: Baby Boy Bragg's mother

CONTENTS

Author's Note ix
Prologue xi

Chapter One 1
Chapter Two 5
Chapter Three 15
Chapter Four 27
Chapter Five 37
Chapter Six 47
Chapter Seven 59
Chapter Eight 73
Chapter Nine 85
Chapter Ten 95
Chapter Eleven 105
Chapter Twelve 117
Chapter Thirteen 127
Chapter Fourteen 137
Chapter Fifteen 147
Chapter Sixteen 157

Chapter Seventeen 167
Chapter Eighteen 177
Chapter Nineteen 187
Chapter Twenty 197
Chapter Twenty-One 207
Chapter Twenty-Two 217
Chapter Twenty-Three 227
Chapter Twenty-Four 235
Chapter Twenty-Five 245

Epilogue 251
Acknowledgments 253
Bibliography 255
About the Author 257

AUTHOR'S NOTE

The character of Eleanor Blakemore is totally fictitious. However, her struggles as presented were not. They are based on those of Elizabeth Blackwell, the first woman trained as a physician in the United States. Her experiences, as described in her autobiography, *Pioneer Work in Opening the Medical Profession to Women*, were pivotal in creating Eleanor Blakemore's interaction with the medical profession in this work of fiction.

PROLOGUE

Philadelphia, 1847

Inside her head, beneath her calm demeanor, Eleanor Blakemore was screaming at the familiar words being directed at her:
"If you want to go to medical school, you should dress up like a man and apply in Paris, not in the United States."
She adjusted her corset and almost tripped on her blue velvet ankle-length skirt as she marched out of his office. It was the fourth such interview she had had. The words weren't always the same, but the message was. She rejected this idea and continued to plod forward and seek her medical education in the US, and she succeeded.

Women did not have the right to vote and would not until 1920, more than seventy years later. They, for the most part, did not receive an education beyond the eighth grade. No woman had been trained in the art and science of medicine in the United States. This meant that half the population was excluded from being taught—and subsequently, providing—medical care. Enter an upstart, tiny, energetic woman to change all that.

Over a century later, Eleanor's trials and tribulations were discovered by her great-great-niece, Liz.

Medford, Massachusetts, August 1979

"I found this box of letters and journal notes from the eighteen hundreds written by your great-great-great-aunt Eleanor." Liz Turner's voice cracked through the phone.

"Wow! Where'd you find them, Mom?" Joan asked.

"In the attic of the lake house."

Joan's family had a house on Lake Winnipesaukee in New Hampshire that had been passed down for many generations and was shared by Liz and her brother, John.

"You remember that big old trunk that had a rusted lock on it that we were never able to get into? I found three keys in the false bottom of one of the drawers in the dressing table in the blue bedroom. One of them fit the trunk's lock, but it required graphite in its keyhole. With some wiggling and wrangling, I was able to finally get it open. Among the contents was a journal that consisted of loose browned pages tied together with faded blue ribbons and several bundles of letters tied in the same way. The letters were written mostly by Aunt Eleanor, but some were by her mother and some by her sister Emily. The journal was Eleanor's. Pretty incredible! I think you'd enjoy reading them."

"Sounds right. They're over a hundred years old! That's a pretty amazing find, Mom."

"It is. So, when can you come home and look at these with me?"

"With our schedules, it may be a while. Could you send copies to me?"

CODE PINK

Chicago, 1980

Over a century following her aunt's training, Eleanor's great-great-great-niece, Joan Turner, was a third-year medical student in Chicago when she responded to a "Code Pink."

Code Pink referred to a pediatric hospital call signal delivered through the overhead speaker system indicating a patient had gone missing. In the vast majority of such emergency codes, probably over 99 percent, the child was found in the recreation room, or in the cafeteria, or wandering the halls. Not this time.

ONE

TURKEY VULTURE: *Cathartes aura*

A large black carrion feeder with a red featherless head, often seen soaring in groups. The turkey vulture finds food by smell.

January 1980, Chicago, Illinois

JOAN TURNER WAS SCREAMING out loud ferociously.

Bill Baxter's voice crackled through the answering machine speaker. "Joanie, I think it's better that you not come to Seattle. I've met someone."

She pushed the button to stop the message and sank to the floor. *The bastard! He's met someone. I've met a lot of people. What the hell does that mean?*

She had said to Bill, before he left Chicago last July for his cardiology residency, "You know, Bill, Seattle is pretty far away."

"Only a four-hour plane ride," he replied. "We'll be fine."

His confidence reassured her, but her eyes teared up, just slightly, as they walked hand in hand. He was, after all, "older and wiser."

His leaving had not been discussed much since he decided to accept the offer. Although they had been running together the previous week, little talking occurred until they completed their exercise. Even then, Joan felt the discussion was brief and unfinished. As usual, they had to rush off to their various duties.

His parents had encouraged him. Seattle had a very good training program. They felt that was the most important variable in making this decision. In addition, Bill was from California, and they wanted their son back on the West Coast. He had, of course, talked some with Joan about his decision beforehand, but it had been a one-way conversation. In the end, he had decided on Seattle.

They had been together for about a year. Tall and lean, brown-eyed and sandy-haired, he had appealed to her both intellectually and physically. Ahead of her in school, he had advised her about future rotations and possible career choices, but more important, he made her laugh. She was an only child, far away from her home in Massachusetts, and he helped her feel safe. They had never lived together as such. For the last three years, she had shared an apartment with her fellow classmate Kathy Donaldson. Nonetheless, these last six months, she had really missed him.

Their long-distance relationship had initially been filled with excitement and promise, which had recently waned. She was going to visit him in Seattle. He was going to visit her in Chicago. But things never really came together. Their lives were so busy. Their next plan had been for her to fly to Seattle over Martin Luther King weekend.

Done. Not happening!

Kathy, Joan's roommate, stumbled through the front door, almost tripping over Joan's enthusiastic dog, Rusty. "Hi, Joanie. I'm home."

When she entered the living room, Joan was still crumpled on the floor with tears welling up in her brown eyes. "That bastard! I feel like a piece of raw meat lying on a plate naked!"

"What happened?"

Joan pointed to the answering machine. "He's 'met someone' and doesn't want me to come to Seattle."

"The bastard! You're best rid of him. Let him stew out there in the Seattle fog. Let him get vitamin D deficient from the lack of sun," Kathy said as she hugged Joan.

The two girls sat holding each other and commiserating for a while, and they concluded that long-distance relationships were doomed but Bill was still a bastard.

"I'm going to bed," Joan said as she pulled herself up off the floor. "Calling it a day." She flashed a grim smile at Kathy as she moved toward her bedroom.

Clad in her purple flowered, flannnel pj's, Joan climbed into bed with Rusty snuggled at the foot in his bed. "Night, Rust." She had just barely begun to succumb to sleep when—

"Hi, Joan. I'm your aunt Eleanor. Just checking in on you."

"My goodness! What are you doing here? I mean, you must be a hundred and fifty years old!"

"One hundred and fifty-nine."

Good grief! My mom told me about our aunt Eleanor, but I didn't expect to meet her!

"Just touching base. Let's get a few things straight here. The fact that Bill is a jerk isn't your fault, and he isn't worth any time or angst you spend thinking about him. And, by the way, I'm really glad you're in medical school."

Joan awoke the next morning with a heavy feeling in her chest. She took a few deep breaths, trying to rid herself of the post-Bill weightiness. Then, she sat up abruptly in her bed with thoughts of her aunt Eleanor.

What a crazy dream! It feels like I really met with my aunt Eleanor. She didn't look bad for one hundred and fifty-nine years old.

After pulling herself together, she was in the kitchen preparing a bowl of Cheerios when Kathy, still sleepy, stumbled in. "How are you doing Bill-wise?"

"I don't want to talk about it. He's a jerk, and I don't want him in my mind. He doesn't deserve to take up space there."

"Okay, message received. You're probably right."

"I had this crazy dream about my aunt Eleanor. She came to visit me to tell me not to worry about Bill. It was so real. I feel that I have met her. Of course, the fact that she's a hundred and fifty-nine years old makes this unlikely."

"Joanie, sometimes I wonder if you're wired together well."

"It was a really vivid dream!"

"Uh-huh, I'm sure."

They finished their breakfasts and left the apartment together, Joan walking Rusty and Kathy going directly to the hospital for her rotation in pediatric surgery.

As they separated, Joan looked up. *Vultures circling above. The birds I like least, sniffing out the latest kill with their red, fleshy, featherless heads.*

TWO

BLUE JAY: *Cyanocitta cristata*
A large, crested bright blue bird with flashing white tail and wing patches. These birds rob other birds' nests of eggs and young birds.

January 1980, Chicago, Illinois

NINE HOURS LATER, Joan arrived at her apartment exhausted after a long day at the hospital. Rusty barked when he heard her place her key in the lock and bounded toward her when she opened the door. Rusty was four years old, a brown, soft, fuzzy, and thoroughly enthusiastic Portuguese water dog. Indeed, all Porties were enthusiastic, but this one was especially so.

Shortly thereafter, there was a knock on the door. Her petite neighbor Erin Connelly, a pediatric nurse, stood outside, wearing her crisp white nurse's uniform. "Hi, how's your day?" she asked.

"Full," Joan said, feeling spent.

"I'm on night shift," Erin said. "Can you walk Lily for me this evening?"

"Sure."

Erin lived on the second floor of their three-flat and had a perky gray miniature poodle. The two girls, both of whom sometimes had irregular schedules, shared walking—and sometimes feeding—their dogs. Joan put Rusty's red leather leash on him and followed Erin down the stairs to the second floor to pick up Lily for their walk. As Joan and the two dogs were heading down, they crossed paths with Kathy, who was on her way up.

"Hi, Kath. Be back in a few."

"See you. I'll put on the rice and beans."

"Sounds good."

Following their walk, Joan found Kathy in the kitchen cooking black beans and rice with her own special spices. Kathy's mom was a chef extraordinaire who had carefully poured the culinary bug into her daughter's heart. A chef made a great roommate, but a chef with a sense of humor was priceless.

"I'll get out some ham to add to the beans and rice," Joan said. She was a health food fanatic but not quite a vegetarian.

"Okay. I'll let you spoil my masterpiece with ham, but I'll cut up some banana to add on the side to neutralize the salt and provide our daily fruit."

"You'd better cut some pieces for Rusty as well. You know he loves bananas."

"What dog loves bananas?"

"This one!"

Rusty was already on his perch atop the kitchen stool, watching the food preparation and drooling while anticipating his banana. At sixty-five pounds, he was not a small dog. But he always managed to climb up onto the kitchen stool, scrambling on one crossbar after another to perch for his banana.

Joan was up early the next day, but Kathy, who was on a surgery rotation, had already left. Joan hadn't slept that well. The unwanted Bill kept creeping into her mind. She dressed for her half-hour run, leashed Rusty, and off they went. Her pace was more laconic than usual due to her sleep deprivation and her Bill thoughts, but she was glad to be out and about with Rusty. Running was always uplifting to her, even at half pace.

"Hey, Rust, what do ya think? Do ya think we're going to see that blue jay again today? He's usually on this route." Joan, an avid birder, had been taught by her mother, Liz, who was a history professor at the University of Massachusetts.

Liz had a love of nature and birds in particular. She and Joan had spent many hours walking through the woods, shorelines, and marshes of Massachusetts, and New England in general, binoculars in hand, identifying birds.

The run finished, Joan hopped into the shower. Rusty had had his walk. She had had her run. After wolfing down a quick breakfast, boots and blue down parka on, hood up, gray wool scarf around her neck, backpack in place, she headed out the door for the five-block trek to the hospital. The temperature had dropped. It was twenty-eight degrees Fahrenheit but sunny and not too windy, so an uplifting winter day.

As she walked along, she reviewed her medical school career. At the outset, there were 125 students in her class—of which, twenty-five were women. By mid-second-year, three of the women and one of the men had dropped out. The first two years were didactics, and there was an enormous amount of material, including learning a whole new vocabulary. So it was tough. However, it was her impression that this difficulty was not enough to cause people to leave school. There was usually some social issue as well.

The three women who left were all married at the time they first attended school. Two of them had expressed to Joan difficulties on the domestic front. Unfortunately, their husbands did not like their careers encroaching on their home life, and consequently, the women felt under undue pressure. They reported that there were issues, like dinner wasn't prepared on time or the house wasn't clean enough. Joan tried to talk to them, but it was of no use. They were locked in, not physically but emotionally, culturally. The third woman, Joan wasn't sure about. She melted away before anyone knew. Joan didn't know about the guy's reasons, either, but he had a father who was very eminent in the medical profession. Sometimes a powerful father was too daunting for a son.

Joan felt fortunate to still be in school. It wasn't easy, but she and Kathy supported each other, and that made all the difference. Kathy was Midwest solid, not in build but in mindset. Standing five feet ten inches tall with brown eyes and strawberry blonde hair, she was long and lean. She had been a competitive swimmer in high school in Michigan and still swam regularly at the school pool. As the middle of three sisters, she was quiet and even, with an undercurrent of humor. She and Joan were a good team both as roommates and classmates.

Joan arrived at the hospital doors, went to her locker on the second floor, stored her winter clothes, and put on her white jacket over her navy knit dress. She wrapped her stethoscope around her neck, checked her pockets for her penlight, measuring tape, percussion hammer, tuning fork, ophthalmoscope/otoscope, and mini *Pediatrics Handbook*. Suited up, she took the elevator to the sixth floor and the interim nursery. They were upgrading the well-baby nursery in the women's hospital, so at present, all the babies were here in the interim nursery in the main hospital. The new pediatric hospital, which would house the intensive care nursery, was soon to be completed. She washed her hands before entering the doors. It was always warm and comforting here. The room was filled with clear plastic bassinets on metal rolling stands from which the babies could be lifted. Presently, there were about fifteen babies in the nursery, wearing blue and pink stocking caps and swaddled snuggly in their blankets. Pink and tan faces peeped out with eyes closed. There was an occasional baby crying and sometimes a chorus, but mostly everybody looked very content. Moms and babies generally stayed in the hospital two nights after delivery, giving the moms time to start healing and to learn about breastfeeding plus bathing and generally taking care of their new babies.

Joan was assigned three babies, Baby Boy Marsh, Baby Girl White, and Baby Girl Jennings. Their bassinets were scattered around the nursery. She checked the clipboard attached to each bassinet for the morning's vital signs. Pulse, blood pressure, respirations, and temperatures had been documented that morning for each baby by the nurses. CBC—complete blood count—test results were also found in the charts, from the heel stick after birth. She checked her peds handbook and saw all the values were normal for all three babies.

Joan retrieved the tiny blood pressure cuff from the nursing station and repeated this measurement on each one. In addition, she checked their pulses and respirations and confirmed her measurements were close to those already documented and in the normal range as confirmed by her handbook. She knew how to measure temperatures, so she omitted that more invasive step. She was getting good at this process, and it helped boost her confidence.

Upon leaving the nursery, she went to visit each of the mothers. Baby Marsh's mother was in the bathroom. The OB team was in Baby White's mother's room. Baby Jennings's mother was there.

"Hi. I'm Joan Turner, the medical student assigned to your baby. I'll be stopping in daily to make sure everything is going well."

"Now that you mention it, it's not going well so far. This place has no privacy!"

"I understand. Hospitals can feel like that."

"You know my name—Denise Jennings. This is my brother, Ricky." Denise appeared younger than Joan, very young and very tense standing in her pink flowered dress.

Ricky barely looked up at Joan. His unshaven, expressionless face tilted down as he slouched in the hospital chair.

"Well, I won't bother you now. I'll see you later. You have a lovely baby." Joan nodded to both Denise and Ricky, neither of whom made eye contact with her. *Hmm. Baby and Mom have the same last name.*

Surprised that she was so summarily dismissed, Joan thought, *Zero out of three attempts to make a connection with the moms of my babies. Not an auspicious beginning for pediatrics.* She left the floor to proceed to the auditorium for grand rounds, somewhat discouraged.

Hopefully, this will be more successful. So far, this day is a downer. At rounds, three cases were discussed: one child with juvenile-onset diabetes mellitus, another with a kidney tumor, and the third with shaken baby syndrome—nonaccidental trauma.

She met with her resident, Jim Blakely, following rounds. He warmly shook her hand, and she noted he had a Mr. Rogers gentleness about him. As the two of them returned to the temporary pediatrics floor, Joan wondered whether this was characteristic of pediatricians. He was a third-year pediatrics resident and responsible for teaching and mentoring her. She thought this could be interesting in many ways, for pediatrics knowledge and maybe more than that. He seemed wise.

They were going to see Seth Masters, the patient who was presented at rounds with diabetes. The six-year-old boy had an unremarkable past medical history, including a normal birth weight and normal growth and development. He was in the first grade and had been doing well. Recently, his mother noticed he had started drinking lots of fluids of all sorts—water, juice, milk, anything and everything. However, what was more striking was that he had started wetting his bed. He had been potty-trained since age two, so this was very much out of the ordinary.

She was worrying about her child-rearing skills and wondered whether her son was under some stress at school. When they went to visit their pediatrician, he had drawn blood for a routine workup including a blood glucose level, which was very high, and Seth was diagnosed with diabetes. Subsequently, it was hard to control his blood sugar level with insulin, and he had had an episode of hypoglycemia—low blood sugar—and experienced a seizure. Currently, he was in the hospital following this seizure to monitor his condition and get his diabetes better controlled.

After the required handwashing, Jim and Joan went into the room and greeted the patient and his parents. "How are we today?" Jim asked the boy.

"Fine," Seth said, looking up from his Legos as he sat in his hospital johnny.

Joan was reviewing the chart for vital signs. They were all normal. In addition, his blood glucose level looked stable.

Rapport was just being established with Seth when the ophthalmology resident, Jay Peterson, entered the room. "Mind if I take a peek?" he said.

Jim reluctantly acquiesced, but he and Joan remained in the room. She then noticed, for the first time, that Seth's pupils were dilated. *I missed that. I have to be more observant, pay more attention to pupils.*

Drops had been placed in Seth's eyes to dilate them and ready him for the ophthalmology exam.

Jay turned to Seth. "Hi, Seth. I'm Dr. Peterson. I'm going to take a little look at your eyes, if that's okay with you."

Still concentrating on his Legos, Seth nodded. Jay plugged in a headlamp, which he put on and tightened into place. He held a lens in front of Seth's right eye and shined the light from his headpiece through the lens. Jay looked in and, viewing each eye separately, commented that everything looked normal.

Joan was a little irritated that he had interrupted their exam. Maybe she was taking a lead from Jim. Nonetheless, this guy seemed interesting. He was in charge of his world.

When they left the room, Jim explained to Joan that Jay was doing a baseline eye exam. "We don't expect any changes in his retinas now since he hasn't had the disease for very long. But patients with diabetes can develop abnormal blood vessels resulting in bleeding in the back of their eyes that can lead to vision loss. They need to be monitored for this, so today will provide a baseline eye exam."

Joan was struck by the possibility of this young child losing vision. "Is there any treatment for this?"

Jim said it would be best to ask Jay and winked. "I'm sure we will see him again."

She thanked him for his explanation, and they separated, with Joan going to attend a series of medical student lectures.

At the end of the day, before leaving the hospital, she again went to the sixth-floor nursery to check on her babies. The nurses had just held rounds and changed shifts. Baby Marsh and Baby White were fast asleep and looked content and peaceful, although the White baby must have been dreaming because, as Joan watched her, her little mouth twitched and formed a smile intermittently. *What a cutie!* She checked their charts. Their vital signs and labs were normal. Joan scanned the room looking for Baby Jennings. *Where are you, you little sweetie pie?*

Joan continued to search around the nursery for Baby Jennings, to no avail. *Good grief! What am I supposed to do now? I don't want to trigger a calamity response and have it be nothing, but what if something serious has happened to Baby Jennings?* With a deep sigh, she marched over to the nursing station. Finding the head nurse, Jackie Brown, Joan told her Baby Jennings appeared to be missing.

"No problem. I'll check the mom's room. She's probably feeding her."

Of course. I should have thought about that. Now, I am going to look like an idiot, causing an uproar for nothing.

Jackie came running back to the nursing station. "Call a Code Pink," she exclaimed. "I can't find either of them!"

Joan was shocked by these words. *My first day in pediatrics, and one of my babies is lost! The poor baby, the poor mom, poor me!* Her hands began to shake as the scenario played out.

With the words "Code Pink" resonating through the halls from the overhead speaker system, the protective services team arrived. The hospital was searched for baby and mother, to no avail. The police were called and joined in. While the hospital was scoured, Jackie held a meeting in the nursing station to review the events that preceded the Code Pink. Her face revealed nothing as she reviewed the history of Baby Jennings. "The mom, Denise, delivered vaginally, and it had gone smoothly. She was single and had been alone throughout the process. The baby's vital signs and labs were normal during her stay in the nursery. The mom's breastfeeding training was reported to have gone well. Denise had a visit today from her brother, Ricky. Joan, our medical student, had met them both. Mom and baby have not been seen since. Baby Jennings was noted missing half an hour ago by Joan." She looked directly at Joan as she said this.

It wasn't a friendly glance.

Joan's heart raced as she was asked a couple of questions by the team and the police. She had little to contribute except that she had seen and examined the baby in the nursery that morning and had met briefly with Denise and Ricky following that. She had noted that Denise seemed tense and Ricky was not interactive. In the late afternoon, she had stopped back to visit with Baby Jennings and could not find her, so she had reported her missing.

Where are you, Baby Jennings?

THREE

BLACK-CAPPED CHICKADEE: *Poecile atricapilla*
These small birds have a bold black cap that extends down to and includes their eyes. They travel in flocks and are found in a variety of wooded habitats.

January 1980, Chicago, Illinois
Medford, Massachusetts

JOAN ARRIVED HOME from the hospital totally shaken, but she was somewhat uplifted by Rusty's eager greeting. *Where could Baby Jennings be? I knew something was weird about Denise and Ricky. Maybe I should have alerted Nurse Jackie at that point? I need to pull my head together on this. I need a break. Maybe I should fly home for the weekend.*

Kathy burst through the front door. "I had a terrible time in surgery today!"

"I lost a baby!"

"What?"

Joan recounted the day's events surrounding Baby Jennings. Both girls looked at each other aghast.

"You know, Kath, I think I may go home for the weekend. Replace my Bill weekend with going to see my mom."

"Not a bad idea, Joanie. Clearly a better destination. Head for home and chill out. On to me. I had a terrible time in surgery today!

The attending, Jonesie, dropped a retractor as the scrub nurse was handing it to him. It wasn't her mistake, it was his, but he started screaming, called her a stupid bitch. She cowered and apologized. No one said anything. It would just have ratcheted him up further. But more than that, we were all scared stiff that he would light into us. This doesn't happen often, but there are some surgeons who are just insecure, mean people who have to blame someone else when something goes wrong. They're totally in charge and don't have to be reasonable because there is no one to call them on it. Jonesie's a classic. The nurses get blamed because they are lower on the totem pole and they're women. The male nurses and techs don't get bashed as much. The residents are next in the target track, but I have only been with male residents. There are very few women surgery residents, so I don't know how they get treated, but I'm not looking forward to finding out because the odds are it will be me. Anyway, it was a toxic environment. Okay. I have vented enough."

"No. I just rambled about Baby Jennings. Go ahead and vent. It sounds awful. I'm on peds, and everyone seems very civil, and fewer immediate, tense situations occur there compared to the OR."

"It just shouldn't have to be that way. It should be a team culture with everyone freely contributing to the success of the case. That always yields the best result. When you have a screaming environment, no one dares to speak up and you lose those extra eyes viewing and assessing the situation. Also, it makes it difficult to learn, because you're so tense and worried about doing something wrong. What a waste!"

"There are other specialties," Joan said as she reviewed her recent episode of speaking up herself about Baby Jennings

"It's not the specialty. The specialty is great! You can actually fix something for patients—make an incredible change in their lives. You can be the difference between life and death. It's the culture that's the problem. That has to change."

"I'm sure you're right. It has already changed over time. Good grief, we have anesthesia now. Can you imagine operating without it? Talk about a tense situation. Today's approach evolved from that. It's hard for me to fathom what it took to be a surgeon back then and who would go into the field."

"Not me."

"Or me either. About pediatrics, from my current exposure, pediatricians are generally nice, which helps on a daily basis. You know, how the day goes. It's less stressful to spend your time surrounded by reasonable people. Pediatrics isn't a field that pays well. Pediatricians chose this field because they want to spend time with children and take care of them. That's their driving force rather than a monetary one. Although it would be nice to be paid well for the major service you provide to society. Pediatricians support the health of the next generation, our future."

"Yes, but kids can't vote, and kids don't pay taxes."

They looked at each other knowingly.

Joan did fly to Medford for the weekend.

Liz Turner looked out the window before answering the door, her eyes going wide. "Joanie, how wonderful! I was just thinking about you and, shazam, there you are. What are you doing here?"

"I felt a little overwhelmed and decided it was time for a nice grounding visit with my mom."

"Terrific! I'm so glad you're here. And you came in the snow!"

"Mom, you know I'm a tough New England girl. I can do snow!"

"I was just making tea. Want some?"

"Sure."

Liz came in with the tea, and they both looked out the window. Now there was snow on the ground. As a matter fact, it was still snowing, fine, dust-like droppings occasionally swirling, not the big lilting flakes one saw at the beginning of a storm. The trees were magnificent with the wet snow lining their dark, leafless branches. The wind was coming from the northwest, and the snow was caked especially thickly on that side of their trunks. In the winter scene, colors were subdued, and black and white and grays predominated. All was quiet.

They sipped their tea. Joan felt better already and looked around. On the floor, there were five bundles of decidedly old frayed pages tied with ribbons. Three appeared to be letters and the other two, journal writings.

"These must be the originals of Aunt Eleanor's writings?"

"Yes. I had just laid them out on the floor to organize them. This is perfect. We can look at them together. But how are you? I was so surprised to see you that I forgot to ask."

"Fine, in general, but there are a few things on my mind—a lost baby and Bill—and I had a visit from Aunt Eleanor."

"What!"

"Well. Maybe not really a visit but an amazingly vivid dream." Joan provided her mother with a brief summary of her dream. "More later. Let's look at these now."

Liz untied the ribboned bundles, and they arranged them chronologically, labeling them with sticky notes. It was winter break, and her mom had some time before next semester's classes began. Joanie had the whole weekend. Today, they could stay in their cozy house, listen to Bach, and explore more of the treasures

Liz had found at the lake house. Joan made them a second small pot of Earl Grey tea and brought that into the living room, inhaling the wonderful aroma of the bergamot. Liz had lit a fire in the fireplace earlier that morning, and the room was warm and inviting and soothing with an atmosphere that only a live fire on a cold day could create.

Joan's great-great-great-aunt, Eleanor Blakemore, was the first woman doctor trained in the United States and a family legend. She was one of nine children, the third daughter. The family emigrated from England to the United States in August 1832, when Eleanor was eleven. The journey took about seven weeks at sea from Bristol to New York. There was cholera in England at the time, and several people on board their ship died from this affliction during the voyage. The Blakemore family moved from New York to Cincinnati, Ohio, in 1838, and a few months later, Eleanor's father, who was the sole support for the family, died. This tragedy had an indelible impact on the sisters. The financial dependance on marriage experienced by their own family, and as seen in Jane Austin's heroines in the late eighteenth and early nineteenth centuries in England, was not going to be carried forward by the Blakemore sisters in America. None of the five sisters ever married. The three eldest, including Eleanor, established a day school and a boarding school for girls. Teaching became Eleanor's means of helping support her family and, later, of both gaining access to medical books and earning money for her medical education.

The future Dr. Blakemore implored many physicians and medical schools to consider her desire to be trained in medicine. While reviewing one of the journal packets, Liz found an entry dated June 2, 1847.

"The dean of a smaller school in Philadelphia had written, 'You cannot expect us to furnish you with a stick to break our heads with,' so revolutionary seemed the attempt of a woman to leave a subordinate position and seek to obtain a complete medical education."

On reading this, Joan was struck both by the content of the words and the unusual structure of this sentence from over a century ago. She met with no success in the city schools in Philadelphia and New York, but undaunted, Eleanor applied to some of the smaller schools in the northern states called country schools.

Joan opened a letter dated October 20, 1847. "Look at this, Mom." It was from Charles A. Lee, dean of the faculty of Geneva College:

At a meeting of the entire medical class of Geneva Medical College, held this day, October 20, 1847, the following resolutions were unanimously adopted:

Resolved: That one of the radical principles of a republican government is the universal education of both sexes; that to every branch of scientific education the door should be open equally to all; that the application of Eleanor Blakemore to become a member of our class meets our entire approbation; and in extending our unanimous invitation we pledge ourselves that no conduct of ours shall cause her to regret her attendance at this institution.

She had been accepted for medical training! In her adjacent journal entry, Eleanor wrote, "This letter I afterward copied on parchment, and esteemed one of my most valuable possessions."

She was the sole woman of 113 medical students in the class of 1847–1848 at Geneva Medical College. In fact, she was the only woman at any medical college in the United States.

Joan looked at her mother. "Mom, it's amazing what it took for Aunt Eleanor to get her foot in the door to receive an education in medicine in the nineteenth century. I guess women were astonishingly subordinate to men at that time."

"Many were not educated to read. It was 1826 before public high schools were first opened to women in Boston and New York." Liz looked at her daughter. "Fortunately, we were born in this century!"

Joan's mom had earned her PhD at the University of New Hampshire. She hadn't traveled far from home for her education. Her thesis was on the abolitionist movement in the United States, a topic about which she had strong feelings, both intellectually and emotionally. She was especially interested in the Secret Six, the six aristocratic gentlemen from New England who financially backed the abolitionist movement and conspired with John Brown, infamous for murder and for the raid at Harpers Ferry—both done in the name of the cause. He was a fanatic but a pivotal one.

Of the Secret Six, Liz was particularly interested in Thomas Wentworth Higginson, a Unitarian minister. His liberal views from a hundred years before coincided with hers, and she viewed him as an incredible human being and a true hero. Early in his career, he was described by Henry David Thoreau as "the only Harvard Phi Beta Kappa, Unitarian minister, and master of seven languages who has led a storming party against a federal bastion with a battering ram in his hands."

This referred to the Burns Riot, which occurred to free a fugitive slave, Anthony Burns, on May 26, 1854, in Boston. After the Fugitive Slave Act of 1850, owners could cross into free states to claim their "possessions," and the federal government was required to detain the escapees.

Higginson was also a supporter of women's rights. A friend of Emily Dickinson's, he was the first to edit and publish her work during his tenure as editor-at-large of the *Atlantic Monthly*. During the Civil War, he commanded the first black regiment in the US armed forces. In addition, and of particular appeal to Liz, he was an amateur naturalist, an avid birder, carrying his binoculars and rucksack with him for hikes in the woods.

Liz worked on her thesis during Joan's childhood. The abolitionist movement was a topic of family discussions. In her teen years, when Uncle John, Aunt Anne, and her cousin Adam joined them for dinner, their family conversations often revolved around "Does the end always justify the means? Or does the end ever justify the means?" The antecedent for these discussions was most often the actions of John Brown committing murder as part of the abolitionist movement, but it sometimes extended beyond that. Uncle John was a defense attorney, so he, like Liz, thrived on these interactions. When the two cousins were younger, one or the other of them would often intercede with "You two should stop fighting."

The older generation's response was always "We're not fighting. We're discussing."

The doorbell rang. Liz carefully placed the letter next to the letter pile and went to the front door. Standing with the snow falling on all sides were her brother, John, and his son, Adam.

Joan looked up and ran over. "Hi, guys!"

Hugs were shared all around. The two men stood grinning, snow shovels in hand.

John said, "How about a little help?"

Adam was a history major in his senior year at the University of Massachusetts. He and Joan, both being only children, were more like siblings than cousins. They lived close enough while growing up to have very strong ties to each other. He was home on winter break and knee-deep in applications to law school. Pleased for a break in the paperwork, he joined his father to walk to his aunt's house to help shovel her out.

"Great!" Liz exclaimed. "I was hiding away, wondering just how I was going to clear the path. I didn't want to conscript Joan during her surprise visit."

"No problem. I'm happy to play in the snow with my family," Adam replied.

John said, "Twelve inches of snow on a Sunday is quite lovely. No one needs to travel today, and we can sit back and enjoy the beauty of winter in New England. Of course, then there's shoveling, but we need the exercise anyway. Anne wants to know if you'd like to come for dinner when we've finished. She's got a roast in the oven, baked potatoes with sour cream, gravy, and broccoli. I'm going to make popovers."

"Wonderful! We'll be hungry after shoveling."

"I'm salivating already," Joan said. "Sounds great!"

"We'll be right out to join you."

The two men headed to the driveway. Joan and Liz retreated to the house to change and find snow clothes for Joan. They donned snow pants, boots, sweaters, parkas, and two red stocking hats with pom-poms that Liz had knitted, with matching ski mittens. They went through the house to the garage and found two red-handled snow shovels. Opening the garage door from the inside, they moved onto the driveway where the two guys were making progress.

"How are the applications coming?" Joan asked her cousin.

"What a drag. These things are an incredible amount of work! However, I just sent one off to the University of Chicago, which was more uplifting. It would be nice to live near you, Joan."

"That would be nice," Liz said. "We could all visit Chicago together." She moved over to the front door walkway to start shoveling a path. The four continued for about an hour, clearing the snow and sweating under their winter gear. By that time, it was late afternoon, and the sun was low in the winter sky. They completed clearing the driveway and the path to the front door. Liz and John thought they were finishing up. Joan and Adam, however, who were in their twenties and had limitless energy, wanted to play.

"Just enough time for a snowman," Adam said. "I'll make the base."

Joan said, "I've got the abdomen."

"Cut the medical terms," Adam said, grinning at her.

"Okay, the middle."

John and Liz looked at each other, looked at the sky, and then resignedly but with a burst of energy, walked to the front lawn and started rolling snow.

"I have the head," John said.

"I've got the face," Liz said.

They each rolled out their respective spheres of snow, then Liz retrieved from the house a carrot, some sunglasses, one of her husband's old hats, and three buttons from her sewing basket. Meanwhile, Adam and Joan had assembled the spheres and John had found two sticks for arms.

"Wait, we need a mouth," he said.

"I'll cut a piece of red pepper and get an old scarf. He needs a scarf," Liz said.

Returning with the pepper, which was bright against the new fallen snow, she placed it in the mouth position. While surveying their work, she heard a familiar call: *chickadee-dee-dee-dee*. "Did you hear that?"

"Yes," John said. "Adam spotted him just after you went inside."

"A black-capped chickadee sighting for the amateur!" Adam said.

The four, now quite exhausted, gathered around their snowman, assessed their production, and declared they were satisfied with their work, including the recently added red pepper.

"Time for a shower," John said.

"Agreed," the other three assented.

"Shall we come over in about an hour?" Liz asked.

"Sounds good. See you then," John said as the father and son walked toward their house, shovels in hand.

Joan and Liz returned theirs to the garage, shed their winter clothes in the mudroom, and made their way toward the shower.

"So what's this about a baby and Bill?"

Joan began with Baby Jennings. "Mom, my first day on pediatrics and I lose a baby!"

"Now Joan, that can't be the whole story."

Joan went on to elaborate and followed with a succinct condemnation of Bill.

Her mother hugged her. "It does sound like a bad series of events, but I know you'll be fine. Let's get ourselves showered and dressed for dinner."

What to wear? Liz chose a green cashmere turtleneck that matched her eyes, some black ski pants, and wool socks for walking around Anne's house without shoes. She added her jade earrings, which she had purchased in Hong Kong while attending a meeting, and a long double strand of Chinese pearls. Joan wore what was in her suitcase plus some pearls from her mom's jewelry box. Preparing to go out the door, they donned their long parkas with hoods plus boots and mittens to steel themselves against the cold on the four-block walk to Anne's house.

It had stopped snowing, and the moonlight on the freshly fallen snow was spectacularly beautiful—such silence and quiet majesty. Mother and daughter drank it all in. When they arrived, they were greeted by a roaring fire in the hearth and the smells of roast beef and popovers cooking. Both were suddenly overwhelmed by how hungry they were.

"Joan, it's so special to see you. This is quite a surprise! Hope you're hungry," Anne said.

"I'm starved and very glad to be here."

"I hear you made a snowman," Anne said.

"We certainly did. I have quite the rakish dude with ruby lips living in my front yard," Liz said.

FOUR

RED-SHOULDERED HAWK: *Buteo lineatus*

This small forest buteo, usually found near water, hunts mainly mammals and some reptiles and amphibians from perches high above.

January 1980, Chicago, Illinois
Beverly Shores, Indiana

JOAN ARRIVED LATE, around ten o'clock, from her weekend in Massachusetts, and after greeting Kathy and Rusty, she collapsed into her bed. The next morning, revitalized, she bounded off to the hospital, only to feel the exhaustion from the trip later on in the day.

Walking home the five blocks from the hospital seemed longer than it had that morning. She was thoroughly exhausted. Her bones ached. She heard Rusty barking as she approached the door to their apartment and felt somewhat unenthusiastic about going out again. But Rusty needed a walk, so leaving her coat on, she attached Rusty's leash and went out directly.

"Rusty, we're only going to walk around the block, so you have to do your jobs efficiently," she encouraged him.

Of course, job number one was no problem. Rusty was lifting his leg at every vertical interruption in the sidewalk, fire hydrant, telephone pole, and small tree. Fortunately, he was efficient with the whole package, and soon they were climbing the stairs back up to the apartment.

Kathy hadn't arrived yet. *She must be observing a long case in the OR.* Concluding that she would be eating dinner alone, Joan opened a can of SpaghettiOs, heated it, and made herself some buttered toast—comfort food. This in hand along with a glass of milk, she migrated to the living room and plunked down in an oversized, soft green chair. *Where is Baby Jennings?* Bill thoughts were still hanging in the back of her mind. Too many balls in the air; she needed some answers. Joan was beginning to realize that answers didn't just come—she had to find them. She ate and promptly fell asleep in the overstuffed chair. It had been a long day.

Rusty's barking and Kathy's "Hi, Joan," woke her.

"Hey, guess what? It's supposed to snow tonight. George Hull, you know him, my anatomy lab partner?"

"Yes, I remember George."

"Well, we're going to the Indiana Dunes to cross-country ski. His roommate, Randy Olson, is coming along, too, and possibly Randy's friend Jay. We're trying to get a group together. Wanna join us?"

"Sounds great! A little skiing in the wild is a terrific idea, just what I need. But right now, I'm going to bed," Joan said as she pulled herself out of the chair. "Calling it a day."

After carrying out her evening ablutions, Joan collapsed into bed. She reached to her bedside table for the packet of Aunt Eleanor's writings sent by her mother and began to read from her aunt's journal.

```
I became impatient of the disturbing influ-
ence exercised by the other sex. I had always
```

been extremely susceptible to this influence. I never remember the time from my first adoration, at seven years old, of a little boy with rosy cheeks and flaxen curls when I had not suffered more or less from the common malady—falling in love. But whenever I became sufficiently intimate with any individual to be able to realize what a life association might mean, I shrank from the prospect, disappointed or repelled. I find in my journal of that time the following sentences, written during an acute attack—

I felt more determined than ever to become a physician, and thus place a strong barrier between me and all ordinary marriage. I must have something to engross my thoughts, some object in life which will fill this vacuum and prevent this sad wearing away of the heart.

Oh my. Aunt Eleanor fought falling in love.

Joan awoke the next morning with a heavy feeling in her chest. She took a few deep breaths, trying to rid herself of the post-Bill weightiness, her Baby Jennings angst, and Aunt Eleanor's thoughts on love.
I am getting up and going skiing today no matter what.
She showered, dressed, and found Kathy in the kitchen.
"Kath, I read some of Aunt Eleanor's journal last night. I'll have to show it to you. She fought against falling in love. Maybe she had

experiences like mine with Bill. Maybe she thought the state of marriage at that time was intolerable for women. Maybe she felt being a wife and a physician were mutually exclusive."

"Maybe it's still complicated," Kathy said. "As you know, a couple of the married women in our medical school class ended up dropping out."

"Maybe I should take Aunt Eleanor's lead."

"Whoa! Let's not go there. How about going skiing instead? I am packing a lunch. Ham and cheese on rye for five. George is bringing munchies. Randy and Jay are covering apples and beer. And . . . I've already had breakfast. The guys should be here in fifteen minutes."

"Okay, okay. I'll get some Cheerios, and I can bring chips and pickles. Who's driving?"

"Randy. His station wagon has a ski rack."

The girls finished preparing, donned their ski gear, including wool pom-pom hats that Joan's mom had knitted, and were were ready when the guys arrived. Joan dashed back into the apartment to retrieve her binoculars while the skis were being loaded on Randy's red Volvo.

"Hey, George." Kathy and he had been good friends since first year.

He was an inveterate New Yorker with a photographic memory, a characteristic about which the entire class was very jealous.

"Hey. Meet my roommate, Randy." Randy was in the driver's seat with Jay next to him in shotgun.

"Hey," Randy said. "Meet my friend Jay."

Jay turned to the back seat where Joan sat behind Randy, with George in the middle.

"Did I meet you last week in Seth's room?" Jay asked. "I was doing a consult on him for his diabetes."

"Yes, I'm rotating in pediatrics and was rounding with my resident, Jim. If I remember right, I think you rudely interrupted us," she said.

"I'm never rude!" he retorted with a flourish of bravado. "You're joking, right?"

"Maybe."

Hmm. I'm not sure what I think of this guy.

"I'm going to take the Chicago Skyway. I know it's a toll road, but there are fewer trucks," Randy said.

George collected from the rear seat for the tolls, and with that, they were on their way. The previous night's snow had stopped around four in the morning. It was a sunny day, and the roads had been cleared and salted, so the hour-and-fifteen-minute trip went smoothly. Jay had brought along a Beatles tape, and he pushed it into the car's cassette player.

When the tape ended, George put his arms around both girls. "I have the best seat in the house," he said.

They looked at him sideways and then shrugged.

"Humor me." He smiled.

"Just this once," Kathy said.

"I'm thinking about going into OB/GYN, and I need girl experience," he pleaded.

Again, he received sideways glances and then eyes rolling up from both his companions.

"That's the first time I've heard that line," Jay quipped from the front seat.

"But I *am* thinking of OB/GYN. I know the hours are bad for obstetrics, but what greater joy can you bring than by helping people have their children? I can move my practice toward gynecology when I'm older and can't take the hours of obstetrics. What do you all think?"

"Go for it," Kathy said.

"Wait, guys. I think our exit is coming up. Jay, will you check the map for me?" Randy said.

"You're right," Jay responded. "This is it."

A few minutes later, they pulled into the park.

Joan said, "I have been hiking here in the summer, and there are a lot of really nice trails. Has anyone been here in the winter before? Oh, wait. I see a hawk in the tree just to the right here!" She lifted her binoculars and watched the seated hawk, high up in a nearby oak tree. "Yeah, it's a red-shouldered hawk. They're quite spectacular. Anyone want a look?"

Jay reached back for the binoculars. "So we've a birder among us. That's great! I've been wanting to learn." He raised the binoculars to his eyes. "His back is black and white speckle, and I do see reddish-orange shoulders and breast. What a majestic bird!"

The binos were then passed around among the other skiers as they climbed out of the car. The bird flew and displayed his black-and-white-striped tail feathers for all to see.

Skis down from the roof, they headed from the parking lot toward the nearest marked trail.

"Looks like no one has blazed the trail yet in the fresh snow," Randy said. "I'll be happy to take the lead first."

"I'm next," Jay said.

Joan joined in behind, followed by Kathy, and George covered the rear. They shushed along the freshly fallen snow in silence. It was quiet and peaceful with just the sound of the skis. The leafless branches of the trees were lined with the snow as well, making the whole scene spectacular. Joan moved along in the rhythmic pattern of skiing and concentrated only on that. Exercise always put her in a wonderful zone, despite damn Bill. They continued in this way for an hour or more when Randy came to a fallen branch blocking the trail. He stopped and stepped over the log. Jay took his place as lead and trail maker, and Joan followed him as Randy moved to the rear behind George.

At this pause, Jay turned to Joan and asked, "So when d'ya learn to bird?"

"It started when I was about four. My mom's an avid birder, and we went together all the time. She told me that learning the birds makes you much more aware of everything around you while you're in a natural environment. She was right. You just see a lot more when you know some of the players, like having a program at a baseball game."

Past the log, they skied for another hour or so before gathering in an opening, skis still on, and broke out the lunch. Jay spotted a pair of white-tailed deer through the trees and put his finger to his lips to silence the conversation. They passed the binoculars around. It appeared to be a mother and a teenager, with deep brown eyes and perfect, velvety-smooth tan fur, ears out to the sides, looking in their direction. The five watched the two and the two watched the five until the deer turned and trotted away, flashing their white tails.

George, having taken a bite of the second half of his ham and cheese sandwich, said, "I was serious, guys. What da ya think about OB/GYN? I'm rotating there now, and I really like it."

"George, you can do anything you'd like, so I'd just go with your gut on it. But you may want to wait till you have a few more rotations. I haven't been on OB/GYN yet," Joan said.

"I'm thinking orthopedics. I like carpentry." Randy smiled. "Bones are pretty clean."

This was met with hands thrown up all around.

"It's clear that ophthalmology is the best specialty," Jay said, grinning.

Before he could continue with his diatribe on ophthalmology, Kathy shivered and said, "My feet are getting cold."

Everyone nodded in agreement. They finished their standing lunch and began their return along the trail. Jay led on a now blazed trail, and Randy brought up the rear. They reached the car thoroughly exhausted. Fortunately, Randy had saved a Coke in the car to keep him awake for the drive. The ride home was very quiet as everyone but the driver slept.

Upon arrival at their apartment, Randy and Jay helped Joan and Kathy remove their skis from the car while George slept in the back seat. All concluded it was a great day, and the girls climbed the stairs to their apartment. Joan left on her winter gear to take Rusty for his walk while Kathy made French toast. After Joan came wobbly kneed up the stairs with her favorite dog, all three ate.

"That was just what I needed, both the skiing and the toast. Thank you, Kath," Joan said.

"You're welcome. They're nice guys. Glad we could spend some time together, but I'm beat."

"Me too. I'm going to crash. See ya in the morning."

As Joan was getting into bed, her phone rang.

"Hi, Joan."

"Hi, Mom. How are you?"

"Fine. It was so nice that you could visit. I loved having you home for the weekend, and we got to make it a family thing. Couldn't have been nicer! Did you have a chance to look at more of the copies of Aunt Eleanor's writings?"

"Yes, I did. I read Aunt Eleanor's comments on love from her journal. She fought off love and attraction to guys as if it were a plague. I found it a little disturbing even though it was in tune with my thoughts about Bill."

"I haven't seen that yet. I'm just rereading about her rejection by the Philadelphia school and the remarkable acceptance letter from Geneva Medical School. The Philadelphia letter, in particular, demonstrates how difficult it was for women to do anything but their accepted role of hearth keeper and mother at that time. Thank goodness we were born in this century! And in this country. Even in 1980, there are countries where girls are not educated!"

"Sounds right, Mom. I'm with you on that. But I'm exhausted. We went cross-country skiing today."

"Okay, sweetie. We'll talk later. 'Night."

"'Night, Mom."

Joan had the packet from her mother on the night table, and she opened it to read. She began with one of Aunt Eleanor's letters dated November 9, 1847.

> Just finished copying the notes of my last lecture...It was on Monday evening your letter came—my first workday in Geneva. It had rained incessantly; I was in an upper room of a large boarding house without a soul to speak to. I had attended five lectures, but nevertheless I did not know whether I could do what I ought to, for the professor of anatomy was absent... I had not been allowed to dissect. I had no books and didn't know where to get any; and my head was bewildered with running about the great college building.

Now, first days at any new endeavor are difficult, but this is unbelievably daunting! Joan thought as she compared it to her own first day at medical school. There was certainly a minority of women in her class, but there were twenty-five of them, and they were all friendly. She had her medical books. She was treated like the rest of the class with regard to dissection. She had set up ahead of time to room with Kathy, and the two of them shared a cozy apartment and supported each other from the very beginning. What a contrast!

She thought of Bill and heard herself spontaneously sobbing. She thought about Baby Jennings and sighed. Reviewing her time with the infant, she tried to deduce whether she should have done anything different. She'd felt uncomfortable with Denise and Ricky. There was something wrong with that scene. Should she have told the police about that? The tears had begun to spill over and run down her cheeks.

I'm having a little low point here, but I will manage this.

She lay awake for a while, stewing, but after all the exercise, she eventually fell asleep and slept soundly.

Just before she awoke, in that period of not quite here or there, she was certain she had dreamed of her aunt. She tried to piece it together, to hold on to the dream and bring it into consciousness. No success.

Still wondering about her great-great-great-aunt, she propelled herself out of the bed. Off to the hospital again.

FIVE

HOUSE FINCH: *Carpodicus mexicanus*

The house finch is found in open woods and shrubs, almost always in pairs. The male has orange-red on its head and breast. It is most often detected while flying, giving its distinctive flight call.

January 1980, Chicago, Illinois
September 1847, Geneva, New York

JOAN ARRIVED AT the nursery and looked for Erin. Not finding her, she viewed the ledger of babies in the nursing station. She had just begun to scan the list when Erin returned.

"Hi, Joan," Erin said. "I was just checking the clean-utility room. You're looking for me?"

"Yes," Joan said. "I'm trying to follow up on Baby Girl Jennings."

"No news. The police are investigating."

"Okay. Thanks. I guess I've been assigned three new babies."

"Yes, the ones assigned to you are Baby Girl Murray, Baby Boy Jones, and Baby Girl Patterson."

Joan returned to the nursery and found each of her babies. She followed her routine of checking the clipboard for vital signs that the nurses had taken and repeated them herself to make sure that her measurements were accurate. *On target.* Confirming that the CBCs for each of the babies were within normal limits as well, she cast a glance around the nursery. She really did love this safe, comforting environment. Maybe she should consider pediatrics as a specialty—but the challenge was going to be staying objective, keeping an emotional distance. It was somehow easier with adults. They were less vulnerable.

Checking her watch, she realized it was time to meet her pediatrics resident, Jim. She took two flights of stairs up to the eighth floor and found him at the nursing station on the oncology ward. They were going to see the kidney tumor patient who was presented at rounds. She found him checking the chart hanging outside the room. This five-year-old boy had had his nephrectomy—removal of his kidney—and his cancer was stage one, so he had a favorable prognosis, 90 percent survival. Jim gave a thumbs-up, and Joan followed him into the room.

Oh, great, we're starting with a kid with cancer, the downside of pediatrics. At least the prognosis sounds good.

"Hey, bud. How's it going?" Jim asked, looking at Joey Miller, the patient, but reaching out his hand to shake with the father who was standing next to the bed.

Joey looked briefly away from *Sesame Street*, which he was watching on the overhead television, to smile.

"I'm Dr. Blakely, your resident in pediatrics, and this is my medical student Joan."

"Hi," Joan said.

"We're just stopping by to touch base, and it looks like everything's going along nicely."

"Yes," the father said. "The oncology team just checked in, and Joey's healing well following his nephrectomy. They're getting the next steps in place. He'll probably be going home tomorrow."

"Great," Jim said.

There was a knock on the door, and as it opened, Jay, the ophthalmology resident, poked his head around. "Hi, mind if I stop in briefly?" he asked.

Jim nodded. "We're just about to leave."

"Before you go, please take a look at Joey's eyes," Jay said to Joan and Jim.

The two returned to the bedside and noted that the pupils were especially large and his eyes were shaking rhythmically. *Again, I forgot to look at the pupils. I suppose they've had dilating drops like the last patient, but they are also shaking.*

"You'll tell us about Joey's eyes as well?" Joey's father interjected.

"Of course," Jay said as he turned to Joey and his father. "I'm Dr. Peterson from ophthalmology. I'm just gonna take a little peek at your eyes, if that's okay, Joey?"

Jim and Joan waited in the hall until Jay exited with his indirect ophthalmoscope hanging on his wrist.

He washed his hands before turning to them. "Hi, guys. I won't keep you, but this is an interesting case."

"We're all ears," Jim said.

"Yes," Joan said. "I noticed Joey's pupils. Has he had dilating drops? And what's the movement?"

"No, his eyes have not been dilated with drops for my examination. Joey doesn't have any irises—the blue, green, or brown part of the eyes—so the pupils appear very large. This condition's called 'aniridia.' It's associated with a lack of retinal development. The retina is like the film in the camera. The eyes shake if it doesn't develop fully. In addition, these patients can have an associated kidney tumor, which Joey does have. This is all due to a genetic abnormality on chromosome eleven. Since he was discussed at grand rounds, I thought you'd like to see the eye findings while I was here."

"I'll be right back," Jim said as he walked toward the nursing station.

"I haven't seen this before," Joan said to Jay. "Thank you. We seem to share some of the same patients."

"Yes, we ophthalmologists get around," he said smiling. "By the way, do you have time for lunch?"

This was unexpected, but she did have to eat lunch. "I think so."

"How about twelve thirty in the cafeteria?"

"Okay."

Jim returned, and they talked further about Joey.

"He should do really well," Jim said. "In addition to the early stage of his disease and his good treatment response, his family is rock solid and has been providing great support. That's a hugely important factor that can be overlooked and is a make-it-or-break-it piece. The social aspect of a patient's situation must be taken into account and understood. It can make all the difference."

They discussed this less scientific aspect of patient care, and Jim tried to emphasize its importance.

Joan thought of her family. Her father, Frank, had died in a car accident when she was three, but she had unwavering support from her mother and aunt and uncle. This buoying up counted for so much.

At the appointed time, Joan took the elevator to the cafeteria, which was on the eleventh floor. She didn't immediately see Jay, so she walked over to the sandwich display. *Let's see, I think I'll have turkey*

with brie and cranberry. Quite the gourmet lunch. She reached for the sandwich.

"Not a bad choice," Jay said as he walked up behind her. "I'm gonna have that too."

They each picked up a Coke from the cooler and made their way to the cashier. They paid for their lunches and found a table in the corner of the cafeteria near a window.

"So how are you?" Jay said as he sat down.

"Fine. I'm learning a lot on this rotation. I like pediatrics, but I'm worried about getting emotionally involved with my patients, and I'm currently fixated on one of the babies that was assigned to me last week who is missing."

"What do you mean *missing*?"

"She was there in the morning when I went to the nursery, and when I returned in the late afternoon, she was gone. The police are investigating now.

"Wow! Let me know. I have a cousin who's a Chicago cop, and he may have some information. By the way, skiing was fun."

"Yeah, it was."

"And that hawk was spectacular!"

"Yeah, there aren't so many birds around in the winter, but the red-tailed—and the red-shouldered—hawks are reliably in that marsh area in the Indiana Dunes. When the spring migration comes, there will be incredible numbers of an amazing array of species."

"Sounds fantastic! I'd really like to be introduced to that." He looked across the table at her with such intensity that she lowered her eyes.

"We have a few months to go, but I can keep you posted," she managed.

"That'd be great!"

Trying to recoup her equilibrium, she asked, "So how do you know Randy?"

"We both went to high school in Winnetka, on the North Shore, and we were on the tennis team together. I consistently beat almost everyone on the team but not Randy. His serve was like lightening. He was real competition. He succeeded me as team captain. I went to undergraduate and medical school out east but came back to Chicago for my ophthalmology residency, so now we're in the same place again. We just realized this recently. I look forward to playing some tennis with him."

"Sounds like fun. I'd like to watch."

"I think we can probably arrange that," he said, smiling. "I'd better get to clinic. Sorry to rush you."

"No problem. I'm just going to sit and finish my Coke."

As he walked away, she followed his towering six-foot-three athletic frame topped by his shock of dirty-blond hair.

That was nice. A warm feeling coursed through her. *I needed something like this after Bill. What a jerk that guy was, but I do have to be careful about a rebound relationship. Aunt Eleanor seems to have openly tried to eliminate relationships with the opposite sex from her life. I'm sure her approach is safer, but less fun, and maybe tragic. I don't think I'll go down that road, but I've just been battered, and it hurts. Cautious entry into anything new seems like a good idea.* Finishing her Coke, she headed off to her lecture series, her heart still fluttering a little from the interaction with Jay.

Later that afternoon, she returned to the nursery. Erin's shift was over, so she wasn't there. Baby Girl Murray was tucked snugly in her bassinet, sleeping. The other two bassinets were not in the nursery. Joan stopped by the mothers' rooms and found the babies with their mothers; the babies were avidly feeding, so all appeared well.

She went down the four flights to her locker, donned her winter clothes, and left the hospital. *It's the end of January. The skiing is fun, but I hate wearing all these heavy clothes.*

Walking home, she thought about lunch. Jay seemed like an interesting guy, and he was quite good-looking—not that that was so important, but it certainly was a plus. She'd like to learn more about him. The rebound relationship warning light flashed, but its beam was dimming. Maybe another ski trip would be fun. There certainly was time for more snow this winter.

She saw a pair of house finches sitting next to each other on a bare branch. *Smart move. Snuggle up and keep warm.* She rounded a corner and ran into Erin, who was walking Lily.

"Hey, just the person I was looking for," Joan said, sidling up to them and patting Lily. "Do you know anything more about Baby Jennings?"

"I haven't heard anything since the police left."

"I hope mom and baby are all right. Jim, my pediatrics resident, was just talking about the social aspects of medicine being as important as the practice of medicine itself. This is a case in point. Who knows what's going on? The other two babies have now checked out, and I have three more. I'll try to keep track of these. I thought my task was to learn medicine, but clearly there are other issues to pay attention to as well, like people and their foibles. Thanks for the update. I've got to get home to walk Rusty. See ya."

Once she had taken care of Rusty and fed herself, her bed beckoned, and she was eager to settle down for the night. Before nodding off, she called her mother to touch base. "Hi, Mom. How are you?"

"I'm fine. And you?"

"Doing okay."

"I've been reading some more of Aunt Eleanor's letters. At that time, they were having trouble obtaining bodies for teaching anatomy. She mentions there was grave robbing occurring, frequently by the medical students themselves," Liz said.

"You mean they would go out and dig up dead people?"

"Evidently. They would keep track of deaths, probably through the obituaries, possibly through contacts with undertakers or even through the morgue at the hospital. I guess maybe they also had contacts with gravediggers. They needed fresh bodies for dissection in anatomy labs. It really sounds like a gruesome business."

"Good grief! I'm glad that wasn't a requirement for our anatomy lab!"

"I don't think it was a requirement a century and a half ago, either, but apparently it did happen. Of course, it wasn't legal, but it was a different time. Medical education was just getting started in this country and was much shorter in duration than now, and the profession was more like a trade. Certification and licensure and testing for attainment of knowledge, except in the medical schools, hadn't been established yet. Treatments were primitive. For instance, bloodletting was common. There was no understanding of germ theory. There were no antibiotics. It was a whole different world."

"But still, grave robbing!" Joan exclaimed.

"You're right, of course, but they had to work with what they had, as do we all in whatever time we are living. I'm also glad it is not part of your anatomy training."

"Anatomy is complicated enough, learning a whole new vocabulary. The lab experience has so many dimensions—dealing with a dead body emotionally and treating it with respect, understanding its components and how they relate to each other, and learning the mechanics of dissection. It's a lot, never mind having to illegally procure bodies. That's completely over the top!"

"You're right. I better call it a night. I'm falling asleep," Liz said.

"Me too. Tomorrow's my last day of peds. Then February and OB."

As soon as Joan's head hit the pillow, she was out. There was the early sense of falling. Then . . . there stood her aunt Eleanor.

"Aunt Eleanor! Nice to see you. What are you doing here?"

"I'm coming to pick you up for the dig."

"For the dig?"

"Yes, you know—we have to collect material for class. They haven't been letting me observe the dissection demonstrations. Maybe if I help supply the material, they won't have a choice. I want to learn, which is hard to do if I can't observe. Hop in the car."

"That makes sense, but your plan sounds a little extreme. Do you have permission from the family?"

A look of exasperation was sent in Joan's direction.

"Isn't this kind of thing illegal?"

Another look of exasperation.

"Where did you get this car? They haven't even been invented yet. Where are we going?"

"Lake Lawn Cemetery."

"So what do we do when we get there?"

"There are shovels in the trunk."

"Shovels? Oh boy!" Joan's knees began to shake. "Have you ever done this before?"

"I spoke to one of my classmates."

"Oh boy." Joan spoke in a tremulous voice. "Do you have anyone in mind? Is there a particular site?"

A small scrap of paper was pushed in Joan's direction.

"Plot 546," she read aloud. "Who provided you with this information?"

This question was followed by eye-rolling from the driver of the car, which had just pulled through the stone gates of the cemetery.

"You know, you really don't need to bring me along. I'll be happy to hear the story from you."

"I brought two shovels. Besides, he's heavy."

"Who's heavy?"

"Our study material."

"You know, I don't think this is the best solution to your problem. Maybe you could talk to your anatomy professor and convince him that you should be allowed to observe the dissection demonstrations. This would be a much simpler plan and wouldn't require going to the cemetery in the middle of the night . . . wouldn't require breaking the law."

"I have tried that many times. I need some leverage. This is the fall-back plan."

"It is really dark. How are we going to find plot 546?"

SIX

HOUSE SPARROW: *Passer domesticus*

House sparrows have a gray crown and are usually seen in small flocks near human habitation. They nest in all types of natural and man-made cavities.

February 1980, Chicago, Illinois

JOAN AWOKE WITH a start. *Plot 546? Wait a minute, what's plot 546?* She lay in bed trying to piece her dream together. Gradually, it all came back to her. *Good grief! What a weird dream!*

    Rusty gingerly unfolded himself and stepped out of his bed, which was located at the foot of Joan's. He took a step or two and then stretched into his downward-facing dog pose and held it for a few seconds, followed by stepping forward and stretching his hind legs. Walking around to the side of bed where Joan's arm hung out, he licked her hand.

    "Hi, boy. I'm getting up. Don't worry. Breakfast is around the corner."

    Having taken some extra in-bed time to gather her thoughts, which still weren't completely together, she was now late. She scrambled out of bed, showered, dressed, and zipped into the kitchen where she found Kathy, who was eating a slice of toast.

    "Hi, Kath."

"Hi, Joan. I saw Randy in the OR yesterday. He's getting a group together to go cross-country skiing again this weekend. Do you want to come?"

"Who's going?"

"I think the same five, if you come."

"Sounds good. I ran into Jay yesterday, and we had lunch together."

"Go on."

"He seems like a nice guy."

"I think so too. He and Randy are old friends from high school."

"So he said."

"Randy says he's a really great tennis player and a terrific guy."

"That's good to hear. Count me in on the ski trip. Erin is going to walk Rusty," Joan said as her toast popped up, and she quickly buttered it. "I'm a little worried about her."

Kathy looked at her quizzically.

"She was crying while walking Lily the other day. Not sure why. She didn't want to talk about it."

"She's mentioned money problems to me before."

"Maybe, but I think it was something about her sister. I'm not sure. Last week, one of her long-standing patients died, and she was pretty broken up about that. Perhaps that's what's going on. Death can do that to you. Even professional death. It lingers."

As she left for the hospital, Joan's mind immediately went to her dream from the previous night and then the anatomy lab. She remembered the first day when they were introduced to their cadavers. Hers was a somewhat overweight lady aged around sixty-five. She and her two lab partners had agreed to call her Bertha. The smell of formaldehyde was overpowering, and since Joan wore hard contact lenses, her eyes continually watered while in the lab. Gross anatomy began in the summer, and the old anatomy lab, on the top floor, had no air conditioning. Instead, there was a single wooden ceiling fan, and it was hot! The whole initiation was a little surreal, to say the least.

She had never before seen a dead body. She had an introduction to death when she was three and her father passed away. She had cobwebby memories of her mother crying and explaining to her that he was not coming home. She could not grasp the permanence of it all and kept expecting him at the end of the day for dinner. At one point, her mother switched the chairs at their dinner table so she sat where her husband had previously. Then, his chair would not be empty. This seemed to help them both.

Once the initial shock of meeting Bertha was over and they were instructed on how to dissect, Joan's attention was focused on what she could learn from this endeavor. There was a demonstration cadaver on which the instructor had carried out his dissection, initially the muscles of the left forearm. Each part of the anatomy would then be shown to the class from the instructor's careful work, and the students would perform a dissection on their cadavers. The demonstration body was that of a fairly fit man who was about forty years old. He had a tattoo on the inside of his right forearm that said in script, AS I AM NOW, YOU SOON WILL BE. This generated a great deal of angst and speculation among the students. Joan spent no small amount of time thinking about who Bertha and this man had been and what had prompted them to donate their bodies to the medical school to train future doctors. She, of course, was glad they had, but she still wondered.

She arrived at the hospital, exchanged outfits at her locker on the second floor, and, needing a little exercise, she took the stairs to the sixth floor and the nursery. Stopping by the nursing station, she learned that her three babies would be discharged today. All three were with their mothers, so she visited each mom's room to say goodbye. There was a joyful atmosphere in each room as preparations were made for taking a new member to the family home. It made her smile, and that was not a bad thing! She stopped back at the nursing station to thank Jackie and the other nurses since this was the last day of her rotation.

"Where are you going next?" Jackie asked.

"OB. I will get to see what precedes this rotation, where these babies come from," Joan said with a mischievous smile. "I have really enjoyed being here."

"We have enjoyed having you," Jackie and the others said. "Good luck on your next rotation. Stop by and see us."

"Will do."

Joan picked up a cup of tea from the break room and hurried off to the auditorium for her peds lectures. The last of them was on shaken baby syndrome. Her professor pointed to the X-rays he held up to a light box. "You can see a fresh fracture here and an old one in the left arm, in the humerus, here, and another here." He pointed. "The skull film shows a depressed fracture with evidence of intracranial bleeding. I don't have a good photo of the eyes, but classically, there is bleeding in the retina. These findings are caused in part by shaking young babies before they have good head control."

At the end of this unsettling presentation, she was to meet Jim. She found him outside the patient's room, reading the chart.

"This encounter will be different from the previous ones we have done together," he said.

Joan looked at him quizzically.

"In most patients' rooms, you will find the patient and one or both parents, and maybe another family member, all of whom are fully invested in the patient's well-being. In this room, it is likely that one of the adults caused the patient's illness. Scotty Green has been diagnosed with shaken baby syndrome. The child protective service team has been notified. Let's go to the break room where there's a light box so we can review the X-rays. You can see evidence of old breaks in the bones of both legs," Jim said, pointing to the X-ray. "Currently, the right arm has a fracture of the humerus, and the skull has a depressed fracture. The skull film also shows a subdural bleed, demarcated by this arrow."

Joan viewed the films with a horrified look on her face.

"Let's go see the patient. I'll do all the talking. Try to have a neutral appearance on your face. We don't know the circumstances of how this happened. No one is being accused at this point. Our job is to check on the patient."

They washed their hands and entered the room.

"Hi. I'm Dr. Blakely, and this is my medical student Joan."

Joan nodded to the mother, who sat next to the crib that held a sleeping child.

She looked up tearfully and said, "Scotty's my baby. This is my boyfriend, Al."

Al nodded.

"Has he awakened?" Jim asked.

"No," Mom said.

Jim pulled his penlight from his pocket and approached the other side of the crib and let the side down. "I'm just gonna check his pupils."

Joan leaned over to view them as well. Scotty's pupils were very large and did not seem to respond to the penlight.

"Okay. Thank you. We'll stop by later."

With that, they left the room, and Joan breathed a sigh of relief. This was indeed a different kind of patient visit.

Joan said, "The third patient with dilated pupils."

"We have a theme going, but this one's different," Jim said grimly. "Scotty has not received dilating drops like Seth, the diabetic patient. Unlike Joey with aniridia, Scotty has an iris. He has dilated and unresponsive pupils because he has suffered brain damage."

Joan was trying to take all this in and was feeling somewhat sick to her stomach when Jay walked up.

"Hi, team. How are we doing?" he asked.

"We're fine, but Scotty's not," Jim said, motioning to the patient's room. "His pupils are fixed and dilated."

"Oh, man," Jay said with a sigh. "I was just coming to give him some dilating drops so I could check his retinas. Guess I no longer need to. I'll let the team know." He turned to Joan. "Twelve thirty?"

"Sure," she responded somewhat tremulously as he dashed off to the nursing station. She turned to Jim. "What a sad situation! This baby has not even gotten started on life!"

"You're right. As we discussed yesterday, the social aspects, the family situation, makes all the difference in the world in dealing with any physical situation, especially for a child. In this case, some caregiver was pivotal in creating this medical disaster for Scotty."

"Who could have done this?"

"It is hard to say. Often, the baby is crying. The caretaker feels overwhelmed and frustrated and shakes the baby to get it to stop crying. It doesn't necessarily mean that the perpetrator is evil, but the result is a disaster."

Joan was struggling to let all this sink in. "If not evil, at least out of control and irresponsible," she mused. "Even so, assault is assault."

"You are right, and sometimes it results in death," he said grimly. "Sorry to rush off, but I have to go to a meeting. I've really enjoyed having you on this rotation. If you have any questions about pediatrics, don't hesitate to contact me. Good luck."

"Thank you. I'm seriously thinking about peds. Appreciate all your help. See you."

"Bye." He turned and walked toward the elevator.

Joan went to the white-walled break room to take another look at Scotty's X-rays. Shaking her head, she put the X-rays away and moved toward the cafeteria to meet Jay.

She already had her turkey sandwich, a Coke, and some chips when he found her and sat down at the table. "What's happening with Scotty?" she asked.

"The team's there. He's not doing well."

"What a disaster! I can't imagine it. I hope Baby Jennings doesn't wind up in a situation like this."

"No reason to speculate. We have to deal with what we have. That's complicated enough. I was able to look at Scotty's eyes—without drops, of course. He has multiple retinal hemorrhages, which is consistent with shaken baby as well. Poor little guy."

"How do you approach this kind of thing?"

"It's tricky. You want to retain your empathy, but you also have to survive the tragedies you deal with as a physician. You can't have an emotional reaction every time you have a patient who is undergoing a difficulty. You would burn out in no time, so you need to learn to maintain some objectivity. It's not an easy task walking that fine line. Many lose their empathy. The best don't."

"What about you?"

"I am still working on it. I guess you have to compartmentalize. I try to empathize with the patient, listen to their concerns, and make suggestions when appropriate, but I don't take their concerns on as my own. Keep my problem pile separate. Not so easy to do, but I think it's the best way to deal with your patient's illness. I'd like to talk for longer, but I have to go to the OR. Can I take a rain check?"

"Sure."

"We're planning on another cross-country ski day in Indiana on Sunday. Do you want to join us? Maybe we can find some time to talk?"

"I'd like that."

"Okay. I'm off."

Joan continued to think about the fine-line dilemma, empathizing but staying removed enough to protect one's own sanity. She wasn't sure she could learn to do this. She felt spent by the encounter with Scotty. Trying to move forward, she decided to go to the hospital's library to learn more about the three patients with big pupils, especially this last one. After a few hours, she went to the second floor, gathered up her winter clothes from her locker, and steeled herself against the cold for her walk home.

Arriving at her door, she heard the clatter of many chirping birds coming from an adjacent evergreen bush. She saw a house sparrow fly in to join the group. "I hope you guys are staying warm in there. Sounds like you are having a good time. It's so important to be part of a group, a community."

After climbing the three flights to their apartment and hearing Rusty's greeting on the last flight, she opened the door to a very enthusiastic doggy. "Okay, Rusty. I'll take you for your walk now while I'm still dressed for the outside."

Off they went, one very excited dog and one less-energetic owner. When they returned, Kathy was climbing the flight above them.

"Hi, Kath," Joan said.

"Hi. I ordered pizza. I don't feel like cooking."

"Sounds great! I'm beat. It's Friday, and I am very ready for the weekend."

"Me too."

The three of them had just arrived in the apartment when the doorbell rang.

"I'll get it," said Kathy.

When she had paid for the pizza and closed the door, Rusty was gobbling down his dinner and Joan was sitting in the living room, shoes off and feet up, with a Corona in its chilled bottle.

"Want one?" she asked Kathy.

"Beer and pizza, sounds great!"

Joan said, "I really like pediatrics. I like the kids. I like to spend my day with them. I often feel I prefer children to adults—no hidden agenda, no axe to grind, no secondary gain. They're just about living life."

"I agree with you on that. You just try to make them laugh while you do what you can to heal them. I went into medicine to try to help people. Adults can linger with illness. Kids are so up front, so in the moment. They feel better, and off they go."

"One caveat is that I don't think I would like pediatric oncology. I saw this one child Joey with a kidney tumor who was doing well, but when they don't, I would have trouble remaining objective. I was talking with my peds resident, Jim, about this today, about not taking on everyone's burdens because the load is too heavy. Jay said the same."

"You saw Jay today?"

"Yes. He came to examine the patient that Jim and I had just seen with shaken baby syndrome. Such a tragic case!"

"I'm sure you're right. I heard that lecture today. But . . . Jay seems to be showing up frequently."

"Yes, he does. We had lunch again today, and he asked if I would like to go skiing on Sunday."

"Great! We'll have a good time, but... Randy may have mentioned something about Jay having a girlfriend."

"What? You've got to be kidding me! This guy has been popping up all over the place and hitting on me, which I have to admit, I thought was kind of nice. But if he has a girlfriend, that's a different story. I don't want another Bill encounter."

"I didn't get any specifics. Randy may be wrong. Things may have changed. But... it's probably worth asking about."

"Ya think? Christ! This is all I need. So how do I bring up this topic? 'What the hell are you doing coming after me when you already have a girlfriend?' How does that sound? Or 'How many people do you usually date at once?' Any suggestions for an approach to this?"

Kathy took a deep breath. "I'm only trying to help. It's worth asking. You'll see him this weekend. Just ask."

"I don't know if I want to see him."

"It'll be fun! You should come."

"I do want to go. Going with the group on a skiing trip is just what I need and want to do. I'm not going to isolate myself just because this guy may be a jerk. Anyway, they'll be five of us, so it's not like we're paired up. Oh boy. I don't know what to think about this trip."

"Just come. It'll be fine."

"Speaking of not knowing what to think, I had a really weird dream about Aunt Eleanor last night. I dreamt she came to pick me up to help her find a body for her anatomy class. It was totally surreal."

Kathy looked at her with a sideways glance. "Joanie, you're beginning to scare me," she said in a singsong voice. "On that note, I think we've solved enough of life's problems for one night, so I'm going to bed." Kathy got up and went to the kitchen to put the pizza box in the trash and the beer bottles in the sink. "'Night, Joanie."

"'Night. Come on, Rusty. Let's get ourselves in bed. It's the end of the month. We're between rotations and tomorrow's Saturday, so we can sleep in."

SEVEN

NORTHERN CARDINAL: *Cardinalis cardinalis*
This long-tailed, stout-billed species is found in bushy habitats.
They are the only all-red bird with a crest.

March 1980, Chicago, Illinois
Indiana

JOAN RESPONDED TO Rusty's tongue on her cheek by opening one eye at a time. "Let's see. Saturday flew by and it's Sunday morning and we are going skiing. *And* I have to talk to Jay."

"Are you up yet?" Kathy called. "They're going to be here in a half an hour."

Joan looked out her window. "It's dark. Oh, good grief, it's snowing! Are we still going, Kath? It's snowing."

"No one has called, so I assume we are. All the better for skiing."

"But we have to get there."

"I've packed lunches—ham and cheese sandwiches and Cokes and chips."

"I'll add some cookies. I already asked Erin to take care of Rusty."

"Has she learned any more about Baby Jennings?"

"Not when I last saw her. I'll ask again tonight when we get back."

Joan quickly showered and donned her skiing attire. Placing her skis next to the door, she ran down the stairs to take Rusty for a quick pit stop.

Upon their return, Kathy handed her a slice of buttered toast with raspberry jelly and a glass of two-percent milk.

"Thank you, Kath. You're an angel!" Joan chewed a bite of the toast while feeding Rusty his breakfast, for which he was always grateful.

The doorbell rang, and after saying goodbye to Rusty, the two girls scrambled down the stairs with their skis, poles, boots, and the lunch.

"Hi, guys," they greeted simultaneously while handing their ski gear over to Randy and Jay.

"Where's George?" Kathy asked.

"He opted out," said Randy. "Something about him having a late night. It was his last night on OB and a baby was delivered at four thirty in the morning, so it was a long one for him as well, late and long."

Oh, good grief. Now we are no longer five, so we are sort of paired up. I could opt out now too, but I really wanna go. I'll just have to try and keep this guy at a distance.

When the skis were loaded on top of Randy's car, Jay said, "Kathy, you can have the navigator's seat and I'll sit with Joan in the back."

"Fine with me," Kathy responded, and with that, they were off.

"What do you think about the weather?" Joan asked Randy.

"Fresh snow will be better for skiing," he responded.

"That's what Kathy said."

"We'll go slowly, and we'll be fine," he said.

"So," Jay said as he turned to Joan. "Will we see any birds?"

"Probably not many in the snow, but there is a cardinal in that bush on the corner," Joan said as she pointed to the bright-red bird sitting on a snow-covered bush.

"Great! We've got one," Jay said, watching the scarlet bird as they passed by.

Joan glared at him but spoke quietly, trying to keep their conversation private. "So when were you going to tell me that you had a girlfriend?"

Jay swung around and faced her. "What are you talking about?"

She stared back nodding her head slightly and gave him *the look.*

"Joanie."

"Don't *Joanie* me. I don't want to talk about this now. Later, when we are alone."

"Okay. Can we talk about something else?"

Joan nodded. *I don't want to spoil this nice day of skiing, and I don't want this to be a public discussion.*

Jay proceeded with some hesitation, but he was mostly undaunted. "Tell me about you. Where are you from? Brothers and sisters?"

Joan responded by telling him about her father's death and that she was an only child and had grown up in Massachusetts where her mother was on the faculty of U. Mass.

The car lurched as it hit a patch of ice. They all stiffened.

"Doing okay?" Jay asked Randy.

"Yes, sorry, guys. The roads are incredibly slippery. I'll slow down."

There was silence for a while.

Jay turned to Joan. "Your mother never remarried."

"No, but she hinted about a possible boyfriend on the phone. Apparently, my uncle John introduced them. We'll see. My cousin Adam seems to like him. They may all be coming to Chicago. Adam is applying to law school at the U of C. My uncle John is a defense attorney, so Adam could be following in his footsteps."

Joan was about to ask about Jay's family, but she felt herself holding back. She was not eager to be pushed into another relationship yet. Maybe she had shared too much.

But Jay rolled on. "My parents, Patrick and Meghan, live in Winnetka. My dad is a banker, and so is my younger brother, Alex. My mom is a pediatrician in private practice in Evanston, and my younger sister, Lisa, is in law school at the University of Michigan."

"Professional family!" said Joan.

"So's yours."

"Yeah, I guess that's true."

"What are you thinking of going into?"

"Kathy and I were just discussing that on Friday. I like spending the day with kids. I go to OB next, and I think I would like operating, so we'll see.

"Have you considered ophthalmology?"

"No, but I don't know much about it."

"You've come to the right place," he said with a flourish. "I'm an expert."

"I am sure you are," she countered.

"No, really, it's a great specialty. Surgery is a significant part of it, largely microsurgery. People are very grateful when you enable them to see by operating on their cataracts, and everybody develops cataracts if they live long enough. You follow people over many years and develop wonderful relationships. The hours are manageable for having a personal life and a family. It's worth considering."

"You're a good salesman."

"You should at least do a rotation and make your own decision." He directed his attention to Randy. "How is it going up there?"

"The roads aren't great," Randy said, "but I have a really good navigator."

"The visibility leaves something to be desired as well," Kathy, the navigator, said.

At this point, all four of them watched the red taillights of the car in front of them slide off the road into the right ditch. It was all Randy could do to avoid hitting it since it slowed down as it slid. In trying to avoid a collision, he turned the wheel to the left, but this resulted in their car skidding into a 360-degree spin that careened them across the highway. Fortunately, they did not collide with any cars in their trans-highway travel. However, as they roared onto the median, the left bumper slammed the end of the guardrail, and the impact spun the car around so that its rear landed in a snowbank. Everyone had their seatbelts on, but they all spun, and their heads were jerked forward when the car whacked the guardrail. Hearts were pounding all around.

After a pause of unknown length, Kathy, who was still reeling from the impact, saw that Randy's head was on the wheel.

"Are you all right?" she implored as she put her hand on his shoulder.

He turned his head to look at her, and she was shocked to see a gash on the right side of his forehead and blood dripping into his right eye.

"Oh my God, Randy!"

"What is it?" Jay exclaimed, trying to gather himself so he could get out of the car to help his friend. He touched Joan's shoulder on his way out and looked at her imploringly to see whether she was all right, and she nodded that she was okay. He opened the driver's door and took Randy's face in his hands to inspect his wound. "How are you feeling?"

"My head hurts."

"No surprise there. Let's get you cleaned up."

"There's a first aid kit in my backpack," said Joan. "I can reach it from here. It has gauze and bandages and antibiotic ointment."

With these supplies, Jay applied pressure, but not too much, to Randy's forehead and cleaned the blood off his face and eyelid. When the bleeding had stopped, Jay cleaned that area as well, pulled the edges of the gash together with two butterfly bandages, and applied antibiotic ointment.

Kathy handed Randy a water bottle and two Tylenols.

He smiled up at her and swallowed the pills eagerly.

"Now that you can open your eye, can you see out of it?" asked Jay as he covered Randy's left eye with his hand.

Randy nodded.

Jay then removed his hand. "And no double vision, right?"

"Right."

"Everything else seems okay?"

"I think so," Randy responded.

Jay put his arm gently around Joan, who was standing next to him and appeared sheet white. "You're okay? Maybe you should sit down. Why don't you take the navigator's seat? I'll walk you over."

She sat shivering. Her father had died in a car accident, a momentous event in her childhood. The jerking and spinning of the car elicited a flood of memories. She sat holding them.

Jay then turned to Kathy. "Kath?"

"I'm okay."

He looked at Randy, who still appeared a little wobbly. "Why don't you sit in the back seat? I'll inspect the car."

"Sounds good," Randy responded as Kathy pulled his arm around her shoulder and helped him into the back seat, where she joined him.

Jay went to inspect the front of the car. "It's dented but drivable," he said.

"I have a shovel in the back if we need to dig out," Randy said.

"Don't think we need it."

At this point, an Indiana State Police car pulled up, lights flashing. "Everybody okay?" the officer asked as he left his car.

"Yes," Jay said.

"Are you the driver?"

"No, he's in the car. He hit his head."

The officer leaned into the car, inspecting Randy. "Are you okay?"

"I think so," Randy said, wincing. "We're all medical students. I'll check in at the ER when we get back to school."

"Okay. I'll need to see your license."

"Sure," Randy said as he removed his wallet.

"What happened?"

Randy, with some help from Jay, explained that the car in front of them skidded off the road and he tried to avoid a collision but that resulted in sliding onto the median.

"Yes, the weather is really bad," the officer said. "You have to drive very slowly."

"Yes sir," Randy responded.

Jay nodded in assent and added, "I'll be driving home."

"Let's get you out of here. Can you pull out in front of my car so no one will hit you?" the officer asked.

"Yes, I don't think we are stuck," Jay said as he stepped into the driver's seat.

With the lights flashing on the police car, the oncoming traffic had moved right, out of the left lane, and had slowed to a crawl.

Jay was able to pull Randy's car into the left lane and move with the traffic.

Jay leaned toward Joan. "Are we okay?"

"For the moment. Let's just concentrate on getting home."

"Everybody, watch for the next exit sign," requested Jay. "It's not easy to see, and I'm going to need some caffeine for the drive."

"Up here on the right in one mile," Joan said.

Jay took the exit and pulled into a Taco Bell parking lot. "Everybody okay?" he asked as he touched Joan's shoulder.

She looked at him and, despite herself, smiled somewhat weakly. Heart rates had decreased some, and everyone was beginning to relax a little.

"All fine back here, given the circumstances," Kathy said, holding Randy's hand.

"I'm going to the drive-through and get a large Pepsi. Anyone want anything?" Jay asked.

"I'll take a small Pepsi," Joan said.

"Two medium Dr. Peppers for the back seat," Kathy requested.

They sat in the parking lot, where the snow recently had been cleared, to gather themselves further.

"We can take you to the ER when we get to the city," Jay said to Randy while turning to the back seat.

"I'm feeling better, and that's the last thing I'd like to do. Let's just go home and chill," Randy responded.

"Are you sure?" Kathy asked.

"Very sure," he declared.

"We can have pizza and beer at our place and play bridge or hearts or Monopoly," Kathy suggested. "Then we'll be near the ER if you're not feeling well later.

"Sounds good to me," Randy agreed weakly but eagerly.

The ride home went slowly, with everyone keeping an eye on the road to help Jay.

Upon arrival at the girls' apartment, four pairs of skis were removed from the top of the car, the snow dusted off, and then they were carried up to the third floor and left outside the front door. Everyone shed their outer winter wear on the floor in the front hall. Rusty was not there to greet them. Joan remembered he was at Erin's apartment and called her. Erin said the two dogs were playing and Joan could pick him up later. Kathy ordered pizza to be delivered, two thin-crust large, one with mushrooms and black olives, the other with green peppers and pepperoni.

While getting the Coronas out of the fridge, Joan thought now wouldn't be the time for a confrontation. *We all need to rest and recover. I'll talk to him later.* All four sat, Jay and Joan together on the well-worn couch and Randy and Kathy in adjacent stuffed green chairs, each pair covered with a blanket while they moved into relax mode, just chilling.

Jay's hand reached for Joan's under the blanket. Joan pulled back. Her heart was pounding. Thinking it might show through her chest, she was grateful for the blanket. Jay looked quizzically at her and reached again, but she resisted. Some rules needed to be put in place.

"Later!" she mouthed.

Despite this, the afternoon was spent in quiet comradery with everyone rotating winning the hearts game and each of them having some time with the queen of spades. When evening arrived, all four went to the kitchen and prepared spaghetti with meat sauce and a green salad. They ate heartily, laughing over their aborted ski day now that all were safe and sound. Randy was feeling better by the hour and didn't go to the ER. Dishes were cleaned and the boys donned their winter gear, picked up their skis, and made their way down the stairs to Randy's car.

Jay had lingered in the kitchen and managed to hug Joan and tried to surreptitiously leave a kiss on her left cheek before joining the others, but she pulled away.

"I really do want to spend time with you and get to know you," he said.

"We have to talk. Do you have a steady girlfriend?"

"No, I don't. I have an old friend, but we're not together."

"I'm not sure I know what that means."

"I have and have had friends. You and I just met, and I want to get to know you more. I can't help the fact that I have had friends in the past. I'm sure you have had friends too. I'd better go for now. Randy's waiting. I'll call you."

Again, she gave him *the look*.

Joan and Kathy flopped down in the living room after they had left.

"Well, that was quite a day!" Kathy said. "Pretty treacherous driving. Randy seems much better. I understand why he didn't want to spend the day in the ER, but I hope everything is fine."

"I hope so too. I don't know what to think of Jay."

"You two looked cozy," Kathy said.

"I tried to ask about the girlfriend, but when the car spun around, that seemed secondary, so I mostly left it for today. I'd better go and get Rusty from Erin."

When she approached Erin's apartment, the two dogs greeted her with their hello barks.

Chiding each of them, Erin opened the door.

"Hi, Erin. How did it go? Thank you for keeping him all day."

"No problem. They played and slept with each other," Erin said. "Come in."

"We had an aborted ski trip, as I mentioned."

"Bad weather for driving."

"Yes, it was. How are you, Erin? Is everything okay?"

"I guess. My sister lost her baby for the second time. She was fifteen weeks pregnant. They're not sure about the cause. She was really bummed. I don't know how to help her."

Joan leaned over to hug her. "I guess you just have to be there and listen."

"I guess." Erin took a deep breath. "I want to update you on Baby Jennings. Jackie had wanted to keep things quiet, but it's been over a month now, and I thought I could fill you in. Uncle Ricky came to visit the day after Baby Jennings went missing. He caused a ruckus by slamming his fist on the nursing station desk when he was told the baby was not there. He was demanding to know where the baby was, but of course, no one knew."

"Wow! I met that guy when I visited Baby Jennings's mom in her room.

"Do you remember what he looked like?"

"Not really, dark hair, not tall, a little taller than me, about five eight or so. He was sloppy and unshaven. I might be able to recognize him if I saw him again. Though I'd rather not. He was creepy."

"The child protective team said there is some evidence that there's a ring of baby dealers who prey on destitute young women, some of them prostitutes. They promise payment for babies and never come through with the money and then sell the babies on the black market."

"How awful on every level. Do you think that's what's going on here?"

"I don't know."

They both shook their heads.

"Keep me posted. Thanks again for taking care of Rusty and for the info."

"You're welcome."

Joan and Rusty climbed the flight of stairs to their apartment. Kathy was just finishing up in the kitchen when they arrived. Joan told her what Erin had said about Baby Jennings.

"Oh boy, medicine is so much more than just learning about the human body and its diseases!" said Kathy.

"No kidding." That said, each of them went to their respective rooms.

Upon entering her room, Joan's phone rang. "Hello."

"Hi, Joan. It's Jay."

Her heart fluttered as she sat down on her bed, but her anger also rose.

"It really was a great day even if we didn't go skiing, and I do want to see more of you. I know you are rotating to OB. I don't have many consults on that service, so I wanted to set up our lunch meeting. Twelve thirty in the cafeteria?"

"I don't know the OB schedule yet, but let me check. I will page you if that's not going to work."

"Okay. I really liked being with you today."

"Jay, you should know that I'm just coming off another relationship. I need to take things slowly, and I need to trust you. What's the story with this girlfriend, no girlfriend?"

"She's a friend from high school who's now a lawyer in the city. We went on a few dates back then, and we've had dinner together a couple of times recently. We're just old friends. I'm truly eager to spend time with you."

"I see. Lunch is with me. Dinner with her."

"That's not the case, and it's not fair. I just met you."

"I need to trust you."

"No problem. You call the shots."

Joan lay in bed, reviewing the day. *You call the shots. What does that mean? Who is this guy really?*

EIGHT

RED-BREASTED MERGANSER: *Mergus serrator*
A fish-eating duck with a serrated bill that dives for its prey and sports a "punk hairdo."

March 1980, Chicago, Illinois
1847, Geneva, New York

UPON CONTACT OF HEAD to pillow, Joan's thoughts about Jay were abruptly replaced by—

"Plot 546? How are we going to find plot 546? It is pitch-black out here. And how are we going to carry a casket to the car? How are we going to carry the casket in the car? It's too big for the trunk." Joan fired all these objections in her aunt's direction as the headlights illuminated a sign reading plot 500.

"We'll just count to forty-six," her ancestor, who slowly illuminated the signs one by one with the car's headlights, replied. "Here we are," she said. "I'll pop the trunk. You get the shovels out."

Joan, thoroughly exasperated, stepped out of the car, and went to the trunk to retrieve the shovels. Her aunt left the headlights on to illuminate the plot, which fortunately was just adjacent to the roadside. They both walked to number 546, which clearly harbored a new grave with its pile of dark, moist earth wafting that fresh soil smell into their nostrils.

Joan, now committed to the task, looked around 360 degrees to make sure there were no other lights. It appeared they were alone. On some level, this was good. On the other hand, it was midnight and they were in the middle of a cemetery about to dig up a fresh grave and steal a body. It was hard to imagine on what level this could possibly be good!

They each grasped the handle of their respective shovels, placed a foot on the shovel itself, and began to dig and remove the soil from plot 546. Eventually, Joan's shovel contacted something firm, and they scraped about and exposed a large wooden casket.

"Now what do we do?" moaned Joan. "We can't lift this."

"There's a rope and pulley in the trunk," explained her aunt. "Retrieve those and I'll show you." She took the rope from Joan and threw it over a nearby robust branch, to which she tied it and attached the pulley.

"This is going to defy physics," Joan declared.

And magically . . . it did. Her aunt wiggled a loop of rope under one end of the casket and returned to the pulley. She placed her weight, which wasn't much, maybe 110 pounds, under it, and the casket miraculously floated out of its seat in the soil, up and onto the car roof. She then disengaged the rope from the pulley and the tree and used it to fasten the casket to the car roof, which had a luggage rack.

Joan was dumbfounded. Noting that the only visible lights were still their own headlights, she breathed a sigh of relief.

"I'll drop you off at your apartment," said her aunt. "I can handle the rest. Thank you for your help."

Joan woke up in a cold sweat. *Jeez, what a creepy dream!*

It was three o'clock in the morning. She got up, went to the bathroom, proceeded to the kitchen, and then poured herself a glass of milk and set out a plate of cookies. *I am going to have to eat something and recover from that dream before I'll be able to go back to sleep.* She sat in the kitchen and finished her fare while running the dream over and over in her head.

The next morning, she was back in the kitchen preparing a bowl of Cheerios when Kathy, still sleepy, stumbled in.

"Well, Kath, I had a really weird dream!"

"What dream?"

Joan recounted the dream.

"Your aunt Eleanor really does seem to have a presence in this century," Kathy declared.

Joan looked back at her in dismay. "Presence—I guess that's one way to describe it. I'm going to take Rusty for a walk."

"Okay, Rust. Let's see who's out here this morning. I need to clear my head," Joan said as they walked by a lagoon. "Oh, wow, the mergansers are back! I know these guys. They're super ducks with punk hairdos that dive and catch fish and are faster than the other ducks—and the seagulls, for that matter." She watched as a seagull tried to steal the small duck's catch.

The two birds were having a swimming race, and the seagull was gaining on the duck, probably because the merganser was carrying his fish breakfast along with his own weight through the water. The seagull grabbed the merganser's foot in his bill. The merganser was swallowing the fish and diving, dragging the seagull below the surface with him. The seagull capitulated, let go of the duck's foot, and flew away.

"Well, Rust, that was quite a show. Three cheers for the merganser! It appears that there are interesting birds to see in Chicago, even in March. I'd better get to my OB introduction. Let's head home."

The two of them climbed the stairs to the third floor. Joan took off Rusty's leash and gave him a pet on his curly brown head. "Well, guy, that was fun. You have a good day. See you."

Thoughts about obstetrics, which was her first surgical rotation, filled her head as she proceeded. *There's the sterile surgical scrub preparation. I need some lessons in that. I hope I don't pass out while in the operating room wearing a mask, as happened to a couple of my classmates. They said at first you feel you can't breathe. In fact, the oxygen intake with each breath is lower, and masks can be hot in a room that is already overheated for the procedure. Of course, the big deal is the surgery itself. The initial scalpel cutting into the skin and tissues below, the blood, viewing the living insides of a human being.* Her palms were sweating just thinking about the upcoming events.

She went on her way to the women's hospital, with a stop first at her locker in the main hospital. Her new location was a gray stone building adjacent to the main hospital, whereas the old, temporary children's hospital, where she had been, was incorporated into the main hospital. The new, freestanding children's hospital was opening this week. The three buildings, and associated storage areas, were connected by tunnels. In the early twentieth century and before, hospitals that had more than one building were connected by tunnels for the transport of patients and supplies without having to go outside. Winters in Chicago were cold, to say the least, and the tunnels were used as conduits for medical staff as well. They were often poorly lit, maze-like, and without signage. In more recent times, these building connections were made by bridges joining upper floors.

She met with her resident, Ernie Smith, and the rest of the team for an introduction to the tunnel passage and the new location. This was followed by didactic instruction in obstetrics and gynecology. Before she knew it, her watch read twelve fifteen. The lecture series was over, and it was time to meet Jay in the cafeteria. She descended the stairs to the tunnels. There was a virtual maze of tunnels connecting the hospitals and various sections therein. The signage was poor, but Ernie had shown her the way in the opposite direction, and she thought she knew her way back. She had one misstep, but she heard some classmates and joined them as they made their way back. Arriving at the main hospital, she took the elevator to the eleventh floor to the cafeteria. There stood Jay, his sandwich in hand, waiting for her.

"Sorry. I am still learning the tunnels," she apologized.

"No problem. That's something you most definitely need to learn. They are sort of dark and scary, day or night."

"Don't say that! I am already fully aware of the scary part," she countered. "I am just going to get some yogurt. Why don't you find a table?"

"Aye aye, captain." He smiled back with a salute.

She dismissed this with a flick of her right hand and picked out some Dannon yogurt with blueberries, a carton of milk, and a small pack of Lorna Doone cookies.

She brought these to the table with a sheepish grin. "I am not eating so healthy today."

"Looks like you have your calcium covered," he responded.

"Yeah, that's true."

"How are you?" he asked, watching her with his penetrating blue eyes.

"Still wondering about you, but fine. The OB-GYN intro was good, and my resident, Ernie, was helpful though a little quirky."

"You don't have to wonder about me. We'll learn by spending time with each other. And they're all a little quirky." He winked gently. "I was in the OR this morning closing an open globe."

"An open globe?"

"A four-year-old boy, one of nine kids, nice family, was trying to open a bag of chips on his own with a knife. Somehow, it ended up in his left eye. How is still a mystery, but these things happen."

"Oh, how terrible!" Joan winced as she spoke.

"We closed it. Since 10-0 suture is finer than a human hair and it floats, it is a challenge to learn to suture with it, but I am getting there."

"Did you close it yourself?"

"No, but I placed a couple of the stitches."

"Will he see?"

"Hard to know at this point, but this is his best shot. He probably will develop a cataract and require another procedure to remove it and place an intraocular lens."

"Sounds futuristic—bionic!"

"It sort of is. It's cool, as I said before, and you should think about ophthalmology as a specialty."

"Looks like I am going to have to just to understand what you are talking about," she said, looking up at him.

"Well, I am glad you are interested in what I do," he said, reaching for her hand and squeezing it.

"I am," she responded, looking questioningly into those blue eyes.

"But you need to do it for your own education as well. You might really like it, and you don't want to miss out on a possible career that will fulfill you."

"Of course, but can't I have two reasons?"

"Absolutely, even better! I've been thinking. I would like to see you every day," he declared, looking into her browner-than-brown eyes. "Do you think we can set up a standing lunch here at twelve thirty as long as our schedules allow it?"

"Sounds good, but let's not rush it."

"It won't be rushed. Our schedules are too busy for that."

"I have to meet Ernie," she responded as they both got up, put their trash in the container, and headed in different directions.

Joan took the elevator to the basement and threaded the dystopian tunnel system back to the women's hospital without a misstep. *Whew, I think I've got this one down now.* She took the stairs to the fourth floor where she met Ernie in the delivery unit.

"Joan, you should go to the nursing station and get your assigned locker info and scrubs, and I will meet you in OR 2. Also, be sure to put on shoe covers and a hat. The masks are outside the OR room near the scrub sinks." Joan followed his instructions and, attired in blue scrubs and paper booties, shuffled to OR 2 where she saw the masks. When she entered the room, she found Ernie, who was hard to recognize at first beneath his surgical attire. The two of them proceeded to the OR to check on a C-section patient.

Joan had experienced no small amount of angst anticipating her first day in surgery, and now she was here. *Okay, the damn mask is on. I'm scrubbed. In the room. Crap! I'm having trouble breathing.* Her breaths came rapidly. *My ears are beginning to ring.*

Ernie looked over, noticing the pallor above her mask. "Breathe with your mouth open when you have a mask on," he quietly ordered.

She did this, and in a few moments, her breathing slowed and she felt more comfortable. The patient was prepped, and the drapes were put in place. Gloved hands were pulling the skin taught in preparation for the scalpel. The scalpel entered, and red oozed along its linear path. First layer.

Shit, I'm gonna lose it. I know I'm gonna lose it. Maybe if I can look next to the wound so I appear attentive but don't watch it directly, I'll be okay. With a little time and a few breaths, she was.

I got through my first surgical procedure—not sterling but still standing.

Joan was ripped out of her concentration by "We'd better check on the other patient."

She turned to Ernie. They both removed their gloves and scrub gowns, and the two of them walked out of the delivery room and into the labor suite. As he was examining Sarah, who was on her own and having her first baby, Ernie pointed out to Joan that Sarah was eight millimeters dilated and almost fully effaced. They watched the heart monitor, and it dipped to ninety-nine.

Ernie touched Sarah's hand and said, "It won't be long now." He motioned to Joan to leave the room with him. "We have to call Dr. Cornell. I don't like that heart rate," he said with quiet urgency. "We don't want the baby to become hypoxic."

They found Dr. Cornell just leaving the OR suite. Ernie explained his concern, and Dr. Cornell proceeded immediately to Sarah's bedside.

While moving in that direction, he turned to Ernie and said, "Tell the nurses we may need to prepare for a C-section." After doing this, they followed Dr. Cornell's path to the labor suite and arrived just as he was leaving. The orderly had rolled the cart in and was about to move Sarah to delivery. Joan and Ernie donned their masks and headed toward the delivery room as well.

There was action all around. The table was being prepared, and instrument sterile packs and trays were out but not yet opened. A prep tray was set up with betadine antiseptic being poured into a metal cup, and gauze packs were opened. The anesthesiologist checked his gas tanks and opened a sterilized mask to deliver the anesthetics to the patient. Urgent action with careful attention to detail filled the room. Outside the door, Dr. Cornell scrubbed his hands and forearms with betadine. Overlying this frenetic activity was a deliberate and calm exterior.

Ernie looked to him as they walked by the scrub sink to enter the room. "Do you want me to scrub in?"

"Yeah, both of you can, but let's move on this," he urged.

When they joined him, he was seated at Sarah's feet, which were in the stirrups.

Following his exam, he concluded, "She's progressed. We're going with a vaginal delivery."

Whew, one C-section on my first day was enough. Now I get to see a vaginal delivery, no scalpel. Joan sighed.

Ernie stood near Dr. Cornell on his right, ready to assist; the nurse was on his left, and Joan was at Ernie's right shoulder positioned to be able to observe. The head was crowning. Dr Cornell deftly performed the episiotomy to extend the opening of the birth canal and avoid tearing of the tissues.

Joan watched in awe as the head was delivered face down and then rotated clockwise and the nose and mouth were suctioned. *My goodness, another person, a new, perfect person is coming into this world. It's hard to get my mind around the awesomeness of this event.*

The shoulders were delivered one at a time, and then the rest of the body slipped out smoothly. Ernie was holding the baby below Sarah to allow for blood to flow into the newborn before the cord was clamped. All smiled and breathed a sigh of relief when they heard the baby cry out for the first time. Cheers erupted!

"Lungs are working," Dr. Cornell said, smiling beneath his mask.

After the cord was cut and clamped, Ernie passed the baby to the nurse, who placed her in the bassinet to clean her for the pediatrician's exam. The pediatrician completed his exam, saying, "APGAR of nine, ten fingers and ten toes, all seems in order, a beautiful baby girl!"

Dr. Cornell was expelling the placenta as the baby was handed to Sarah for feeding.

"Eat up," he said. "You've had a long and arduous journey coming into this world!"

Ernie stitched up the episiotomy as Joan watched.

The whole event is utterly surreal. Suddenly . . . there is another person in the room!

Sarah was breastfeeding the newborn as Ernie wheeled them out of the room.

"Happy ending!" said Joan to Ernie, who smiled back at her.

They met in the breakroom, and Ernie reviewed the steps of the delivery for Joan.

"A truly miraculous process," she said as she tried to express her wonder to Ernie.

He smiled and replied, "It's the joy of obstetrics. We all feel it. Not always smooth, but as long as you have a healthy baby and mother in the end, all anxiety felt during the process ceases to exist. It's a real high. Let's go touch base with Sarah in recovery," he said. "She's all by herself."

"Hi, Sarah. How are you two doing?" Ernie asked.

Sarah smiled weakly, exhausted from the delivery.

"We wanted to check in with you. You just rest and take care of that baby. No problems? Any questions?"

Sarah shook her head and looked down at her new baby feeding avidly.

"Okay. I'll stop by later."

Joan asked him whether he was going back to the main hospital, which he was. "Great!" she responded. "Can I walk with you?"

NINE

AMERICAN CROW: *Corvus brachyrhynchos*

The crow's large size, black plumage, short tail, and broad wings distinguish it from all other birds. Crows have been associated with death and mourning.

March 1980, Chicago, Illinois

THAT NIGHT, BOTH Kathy and Jay were working late in the OR, so when Joan climbed into bed, she called her mother.

"Hi, Joan."

"Hi, Mom, how are you?"

"Fine, how about you?"

"Lots has happened since we last talked. You had told me about grave robbing during Aunt Eleanor's time. Since then, I've had an incredible dream about her coming to pick me up in her car so that we could go grave robbing together. It was shockingly real and a little bit scary."

"*Her car* . . . in the eighteen hundreds!"

"I know, I know. It was a dream. There were several unexpected happenings. That wasn't the only one."

"As we discussed," her mother said, "medicine was very different then. I have been reading further about Aunt Eleanor's time. There was no germ theory but instead something called miasma theory. This theory suggested that the cause of the bubonic plague and cholera was 'poisonous vapors from foul smells.' There was a cholera epidemic in London in 1831, the year before the Blakemore family crossed the Atlantic on a ship to New York. There were several deaths due to cholera that occurred during the passage among those aboard their ship."

Liz continued. "There were subsequent outbreaks in 1832 and 1849. John Snow, an obstetrician in London, made a chart of where the cases were occurring and concluded that many appeared to occur near a water pump on Broad Street. At that time, there was no indoor plumbing, and in the cities, people did not have individual wells. Rather, they used communal pumps for their water and had to come and get their daily supply from these. Snow wrote treatises in 1849 and 1854, following each of the outbreaks, that described an association between the spread of cholera and the water pump. Eleanor graduated from medical school in 1848 so would not have been taught this, but I suspect she learned of it during her career."

"Interesting that an obstetrician made that observation. I am on OB as of today."

"How is it?"

"Just got started, but looks like it has potential for me. The only downside so far is walking through the tunnel between the hospitals."

"How so?"

"It's just dank and dark and creepy." Joan changed the subject. "Upbeat news. I've met someone. Jay. He's an ophthalmology resident, and he seems interesting, but I don't quite know what I think about him yet." She told her mother about the one and a half ski trips and their meeting for lunches.

Liz listened with great interest—wanting, of course, for her daughter to be personally happy as well as have a fulfilling career—but she expressed a little worry about the rebound issue. The breakup with Bill had happened not long ago.

Eyelids were getting heavy on both ends of the phone line, so they wished each other love and a good night, and both promptly laid back on their pillows and fell fast asleep.

The next day was Joan's second on OB. She was unable to find a companion for traveling the tunnel, but she proceeded through without incident. After attending her morning lectures, she received a page from Jay saying he couldn't make lunch today, so she grabbed some yogurt and a carton of milk on the run and ate in the OB break room.

Ernie popped his head around the corner to say, "We have two patients in labor now. One just arrived. The other has been here about six hours and is fully dilated and effaced, so she will be going to delivery soon. She has had an epidural—a form of local anesthesia—and is quite comfortable. Her husband is with her, and he has his camera in hand ready to document the whole thing. Let's go talk to her."

Joan hurried to join him.

"Hi, Mrs. Meadows. I'm one of the residents, Dr. Smith, and this is my medical student Joan. How are you?"

"Fine now," she gushed. "Boy, does that epidural make a difference!" And then, "Call me Beverly."

"Okay. Will do. Yes, they are helpful."

"This is my husband, Tom," she said as he pushed the curtain aside to join them.

Ernie and Joan each shook the hand without the camera.

"I see you are well-prepared," said Ernie.

"Yes," Tom said. "This is our first!"

"The beginning of a wonderful journey," responded Ernie, who had a two-year-old boy of his own. "I think you are just about ready to go into delivery. Your attending, Dr. Cornell, should be by in a minute to talk to you. Then they will wheel you in. Joan and I are going to get changed, and we will see you in there."

They left the curtained enclosure and moved toward the locker room.

"Joan, I will meet you in OR 2."

When she entered the delivery room, she found Ernie, who was again hard to recognize at first beneath his surgical attire—scrubs, hat, booties, mask. Only his eyes were visible. He instructed her to stand near the wall to observe but be out of the fray. As she looked around at the frenetic activity, she was glad for this instruction.

Beverly was lying covered in green sheets up to her neck. Her feet were in stirrups, and there was a tent of sheets from her waist to over her knees that was propped up to allow access and viewing by the obstetrician who was seated at her feet. The anesthesiologist was at Beverly's head and comforting her. A nurse was standing to one side of the attending, and Ernie was on his other side. Tom Meadows was leaning against the wall next to Joan with the camera in his right hand.

Suddenly, Joan heard a thud as Tom dropped his camera and slid down the wall.

"Are you all right?" she asked, looking at his pasty, sweating forehead.

His eyes were closed, and he did not respond.

Good grief! What am I supposed to do? No one else had noticed.

Their attention was focused on Beverly, who called out, "Tom, are you ready to photo this?"

When Tom did not answer, Ernie glanced over and saw him supine on the floor.

"He'll be right back, Beverly. He had to go to the bathroom. Just concentrate on pushing when Dr. Cornell instructs you," Ernie said and then turned and mouthed to Joan, "Get a nurse."

Joan had put a towel under Tom's head and noted he had shallow breathing and a rapid pulse. She was able to lean out the door and wave a passing nurse into the room. They both saw that Tom was coming around to consciousness but still very pale. The nurse went just outside the door to get some water, which Tom sipped slowly after they had gingerly slid him up against the wall.

"Put your head forward on your knees," the nurse instructed.

There was, of course, a great deal of activity in the room at this point. Tom was still decidedly woozy. Beverly was shouting for him between contractions.

He responded weakly to her that he was right there but looked like he was going to lose his lunch. Joan and the nurse each took an arm, eased him up, walked him out of the room to a chair outside the door, and again placed his head down on his knees. Joan agreed to stay with him. She took his pulse, which had begun to slow. Gradually, the color came back into his face, and he stopped sweating. Just when he was feeling better, they heard a baby cry from the delivery room.

Tom looked aghast. "I missed it. Beverly is going to be furious."

"Are you feeling better?" asked Joan. "Let's see if you can stand."

He stood slowly, and when the wobble had gone, they both returned to the room.

"Now, you get to see the best part, the baby," Joan said. "You can film the first few minutes of her life in our world."

"Her. Wow!" Tom said.

When they entered the room, the nurse was wrapping the baby in a blanket to prepare to hand her to Beverly.

Tom picked up his Nikon camera, which was no worse for wear, and walked over to kiss and film his two girls as the gurney was rolled out to the recovery room.

Joan walked over to Ernie. "Missed that one but had my own excitement."

"Yes, you did. It was very helpful that you could take care of Tom. And . . . believe it or not, there will be other deliveries."

"I'm sure you're right."

"It's late. Why don't you call it a day? I'll see you tomorrow."

"Sounds good. I'm beat," Joan said. "Too much excitement!" As she strolled back to the OR locker room to drop her scrubs in the laundry and dress for home, she realized how relieved she was that on her second day in the OR, she wasn't overcome with being there, so she could actually help someone else. She descended the stairs to the basement and the tunnel to get back to the main hospital, where her locker held her outside garb. While on the stairs, she reviewed her tunnel path to make sure she didn't get lost. She had not traveled far in the tunnel when she heard footsteps behind her. They were heavy, not like those of a woman but more likely a man.

She shivered. *Joan, this is ridiculous. Other people are allowed to walk in this tunnel.*

The footsteps seemed to accelerate, and this completely unnerved her. She rounded a corner and turned her head to see a dark-haired man staring straight at her and moving toward her. He most definitely did not look like a medical colleague. She increased her pace, and he did as well. Just as she was about to break into a run, she rounded another corner and there was George, who had finished his OB rotation but had stopped back to visit.

Joan ran up and slipped her arm through George's, audibly sighing as she did so.

George looked at her. "You okay?"

"Yeah, fine. I just don't like the tunnel system."

"You're right. It's sort of creepy."

"My thoughts precisely."

They walked arm in arm until Joan left him to climb the stairs and retrieve her coat from her locker. After making her way home, she was greeted by Rusty.

"Hi, Rust. How was your day?" she asked as she tousled the hair on his head. "Let's go for a run!" She changed into her running clothes, placed the leash on Rusty, and off they went.

They were running in their respective zones by the lagoon when she was jolted by the loud cawing of an overhead crow. "Jeez," she complained to Rusty. "Sometimes those guys are jarring."

They rounded a corner, and the path moved closer to the border of the lagoon.

I hope it doesn't get too muddy.

At that moment, she noticed something bobbing in the water near the shoreline. She was puzzled. *What is that?* Then the awful truth dawned on her. It was a body, the bloated body of a woman partially clothed in a flowered dress.

"Oh my God!" she uttered out loud in a trembling voice. "Rusty, come! We have to get out of here!" They ran at top speed back to their building and up the stairs.

Breathless and shaking, Joan closed the door behind her and locked it. She felt nauseated but dashed to the telephone and dialed 911.

"There is a woman's body floating in the lagoon," she blurted out as soon as someone answered.

Further information was exchanged, including Joan's telephone number and address. She was assured the police would investigate and call on her for an official statement.

She hung up the phone and flopped into the nearest chair, feeling totally wilted. She reviewed every step of her run, trying to grasp what had happened.

Kathy was going to be home late tonight, so Joan phoned Jay to try to ground herself. He volunteered to come right over. She remained glued to the chair until he arrived. When the doorbell rang, she ran to it, calling Jay's name and looking carefully through the peephole.

Bursting through the door, he hugged her. "Oh, Joanie, how are you?" He eased her into a chair and went to the kitchen to get himself a beer and her a cup of tea.

When he returned, she was on the couch.

"That poor woman!" she said.

He joined her on the couch, and she recounted the events of the evening.

"What happened? I wonder if she committed suicide. I think she was young, though I didn't look carefully. I was too shocked and scared. Maybe someone attacked her? Why? And now the police will be coming to take an official statement. I just spoke to the police not that long ago about Baby Jennings." She moaned. "Good grief! What next!"

"I'm happy to stay with you," Jay said putting his arm around her.

"I'd appreciate that." *I may not be sure about you, but I am sure I want you here right now.*

At this point, the doorbell rang. Two blue-clad policemen had arrived to question Joan. Jay offered them tea, which they gladly accepted. Joan asked them with trepidation whether they had found the body, and they answered affirmatively. She reviewed the path of her run with Rusty and her observations. The policemen had a few questions, which she answered. The interview concluded, and they said they might need more information as the investigation moved forward. She agreed to help in any way she could, and they went on their way. She breathed a sigh of relief as they went out the door.

As they were descending the stairs, Kathy was ascending. She entered the apartment with a startled look on her face. "Is everything all right?" she asked. "We usually don't have visits from the police!" She poured herself a glass of milk and joined them in the living room.

Joan reviewed the evening's events for the third time. Thankfully, she was feeling less shaken as the night wore on.

The three of them continued to speculate on who the victim was. What was her life like? Did someone kill her? Was it an accident? Had she committed suicide? What happened to this poor person to have her body end up in the lagoon?

"No matter what the circumstances, not a good result," Jay declared.

The girls nodded in agreement.

Joan turned to Jay. "Would you mind staying with us tonight? I'm still more than a little rattled."

"I'm thoroughly creeped out just hearing about it, never mind finding the body while on a twilight run." Kathy shuddered.

"I'm in," Jay said. "I'm not exactly eager to walk home in the dark right now."

TEN

EASTERN TOWHEE: *Pipilo erythrophthalmus*
Smaller and more slender than the robin it remotely resembles, but their reddish color is confined to the sides of the breast. Often found in dense brush, where these birds scratch noisily.

March 1980, Chicago, Illinois

JAY DID SPEND the night, initially on the couch and then on pillows on Joan's bedroom floor, next to Rusty. Finally, while Joan slept, he slipped into her bed, lying on top of the sheet and under the blanket.

Joan woke first, due to Rusty licking her face. She puzzled at seeing Jay resting peacefully next to her and then, waking further, she smiled. Despite her doubts, it felt comfortable to have him there. *Good grief, last night was horrific! So glad I'm right here, right now. I can probably snuggle up to his back without waking him.* She lay there quietly, feeling the warmth of his body next to hers. *Maybe I just have to be cautious. I really want to see if this can work. I'm really attracted to this guy.*

She slid quietly out of her side of the bed, leaving him still lightly snoring, and tiptoed into the bathroom for her shower. Rusty followed, and she closed the door behind him.

"Well, Rusty, do we like our new guest?" she whispered. *I do.*

She showered and dressed and returned to the bedroom.

Jay was stretching awake. "I hope you didn't mind?" he asked, looking sheepish.

"Actually, it was a great comfort to find you here this morning. Every time I think of last night," she said, shuddering, "my knees start to shake. I have to say, I'm really glad you're in our apartment with me."

"I'm very glad to be here right next to you," he said while walking toward her.

He gave her a warm hug and then leaned his face toward hers as she looked up in his direction. They met each other's lips and kissed long and hard. They continued until Rusty nudged Joan's leg.

"Do you have to go out?" she asked her dog, whose tail was wagging wildly. Still in Jay's arms, she turned to him. "I have my answer. I better let him out. Do you want to take a shower?"

"Love to," he said, followed by another kiss.

Joan's whole being felt exhilarated. She lingered with this feeling, trying to ward off doubts. The two separated as she went to the living room with Rusty and Jay moved toward the bathroom.

She heard Kathy in the kitchen. "I'm going to let Rusty pee. Be right back. Jay is in the shower."

Upon her return, she faced a smiling Kathy. "So how are you?" Kathy asked expectantly.

"Fine." Joan looked up, beaming.

"Looks like the night was a good thing."

"Uh-huh, a very good thing. I think I just have to trust."

"I'll keep my ear to the ground as well," Kathy said with a wink.

A minute later, Jay ambled into the kitchen.

Joan glanced up from her cereal bowl. "Cheerios or toast? That's this morning's breakfast menu."

"I'll take Cheerios," he said as he poured the cereal into his bowl.

"Morning," Kathy said. "Quite the night last night!"

Jay nodded in agreement, looking at Joan. "In many ways," he said, eyes glimmering.

"I'm on my way. See you two," Kathy said as she opened the door.

"Bye, Kathy," they said simultaneously.

Turning to Jay, Joan said, "I have to go to my lecture."

"I'll walk with you," Jay said as he squeezed her shoulders.

They bid Rusty goodbye and descended the stairs. They walked hand in hand, enjoying the morning air and the sweet singing of many different birds.

Joan tilted her head. "Did you hear that?"

"What?"

"That call that sounds like 'drink your tea'? There it is again."

Jay listened. "I guess."

"Look on the lower right branch of that maple. It's an eastern towhee. They are black birds with white breasts flanked by brick red. They have white tips on the outer tail feathers. They're a little smaller than a robin. That's the first one I have seen this year. Spring is definitely coming!"

"Great! Thanks for that introduction. I'll look for the towhee."

They were at the main hospital. Jay proceeded to the eye clinic, and Joan walked toward the lecture hall.

Jay turned to her. "See you at twelve thirty?"

"I'll be there."

The first lecture was on vaginal delivery, followed by one on C-section. Joan had already seen each of these procedures, which helped greatly with her understanding and her degree of interest. She had a good morning, and it was lunchtime before she knew it.

On her way to the cafeteria, she ran into Ernie.

"Hi, Joan. I just visited Sarah and her baby. The baby's bilirubin is high. She may have to stay longer."

"Thanks for the update. I'm going to see them right after lunch."

"Okay. See ya."

When Joan reached the cafeteria, Jay already had secured a table, so she quickly found a sandwich and a Coke.

"Hi. How was your morning?'

"Interesting. I had lectures on the procedures I saw yesterday, so they were especially relevant. Yesterday was so surreal. It literally went from birth to death. You know about the latter part. I was so overwhelmed by that, that I didn't mention to you how wonderful my experience was earlier in the day in OB. I have now witnessed three births, one by C-section and two vaginal deliveries. It was such an uplifting experience that it makes me think about going into OB-GYN."

"It's good to have a positive attitude. Last month, you were high on pediatrics."

"You're right. I do like most of my rotations while I am on them, and that's a good thing."

"Enjoy them while you're there. Consider each. Then, when you are finished, compare the experiences to make your decision."

"Good advice, I am sure. How was your morning?"

"Nothing special. Clinic went fine. A more relevant question is how was my night?" he said, fixing his eyes directly on hers.

"It was very comforting that you could stay with us, Jay."

"Comforting? Is that all?"

"No, of course not."

Ernie walked up. "Are you going to see Sarah soon?"

"Yes, we were just finishing," Joan said, relieved she would have a companion in the tunnel. "Have you met Jay? He's an ophthalmology resident."

Jay's eyebrows arched as if to say, *I assumed I was more than just an ophthalmology resident*. But he smiled and reached out to Ernie for a handshake.

"Ernie is my OB resident. We were together in the delivery room yesterday."

"Okay. I'll let you two go to OB," Jay said with a tinge of subtle sarcasm obvious to Joan but probably not to Ernie.

Joan had told neither Jay nor Ernie about her concerns with the tunnel system and regretted that Jay was not aware of her fears. It was clear that this was not the time to tell him. However, just because he slept in her bed last night, that didn't mean he owned her. In fact, she hadn't invited him.

Jay got up and waved.

Ernie looked at Joan. "I am sorry if I interrupted your lunch."

"No, I am very glad to walk with you to the women's hospital," she said with honest relief.

They made their way through the tunnel system without seeing anyone else. Ernie separated to go to the gynecology clinic for the afternoon while Joan proceeded to Sarah's room.

"Hi, Sarah. How are you, and how's that beautiful baby of yours?"

"I'm still a little wobbly but okay. Anna has a high bilirubin, so she's under the bili lights."

Bili lights were a type of phototherapy used to treat newborn jaundice—a yellowing of the skin due to excess bilirubin. The wavelength of light in this system can break down bilirubin to substances that can readily be removed from the body. Joan recalled that they'd covered this topic in a recent lecture.

"That should be fine. Babies respond really well to the lights. It'll just be a few days."

"Yes, but I'm probably going home tomorrow, and she has to stay. I don't like leaving my baby."

"But you can visit her all day if you want and breastfeed and pump for the evening feeds."

"I know, but I am worried that someone will take her. While I was pregnant, I dreamt that she was switched with another baby in the nursery. I would wake up in a sweat each time it happened." Sarah was twisting a bit of the baby's blanket while she reported this to Joan.

"The security is really good in the hospital," Joan said while remembering Baby Jennings and feeling disingenuous. She thought further. "Is there anyone in particular that you are concerned about?"

"No," Sarah responded hesitantly.

"You don't want to take her with you if she needs the bili lights."

"I know."

"I can peek in on her every day."

"Thanks," Sarah said with a worried look on her face.

"Are you all right?"

"Yes, I'm going to the nursery to feed her."

"Okay. See you tomorrow."

Sarah nodded in response.

Joan paged Ernie to discuss Sarah's concerns about her baby being taken. Remembering the experience with Baby Jennings, Joan realized Sarah's concerns might be warranted. Ernie listened but thought Sarah was overreacting. *Typical man.* They finally agreed that he would request a social work consult for Sarah. Joan thought perhaps more was needed, but Ernie was the resident, and he was in charge.

Joan proceeded to the library to read further on C-section technique. Upon finishing, she took the stairs down to the basement and the tunnel. *I am creeped out.* She opened the entry door to the tunnel and began to sweat. She stood in the doorway looking as far as she could in both directions. At the distant end of the tunnel in the direction she was going, she saw someone. He was walking away from her, and he rounded a corner out of sight. *Now what do I do? I can't just wait here for someone to walk with.* She decided to go for it and walked rapidly along the tunnel wall on the side away from the branching tunnel he had entered.

She was close to the basement entry to the main hospital when she heard footsteps behind her. They began to clip faster as she reached to push open the door. One of the OB residents was coming out as she was going in. She waved and ran up the stairs to the first floor and the foyer where many people were bustling about. She had made it to the main hospital. An involuntary sigh slipped out, though her heart was still pounding and her armpits were wet.

Good grief! I have to figure out how to deal with this.

She took the elevator to the second floor and her locker. After shedding her lab jacket and medical tools, she put on her winter coat and accessories and headed out of the hospital to brave the cold. She thought about Sarah and Baby Anna and decided to see them first thing in the morning. Anna would probably have to be under the lights for two to three days. She wondered whether Sarah's concerns were just those of a new mother or harbingers of something awful, like the episode with Baby Jennings.

Her thoughts went to lunch and Jay. She was a little peeved at what appeared to be his possessiveness, but she had to tell him about her tunnel aversion. She felt silly being afraid in the tunnel and did not like to admit it to anyone, especially Jay. He might think that she was a whining, overprotected girly girl, which she was not. But the tunnel did scare her. Too much had happened lately. She also wanted to talk to him to get his opinion on Sarah and Anna. And currently, she had to admit, it was comforting to have him around.

She arrived at their apartment and, while climbing the stairs, heard Rusty's bark. Dropping her bag in the apartment, she leashed him and went back down for his walk. She had never been afraid walking Rusty, but after last night's events, she was anxious. It was dusk, and she rushed him along so they could return to the safety of their home before nightfall.

Once there, she paged Jay. The nurse in the OR answered the page. Jay was scrubbed in on a trauma case. She could take a number for him to call when he was finished. Joan left her number and thanked the nurse.

Kathy was unlocking the door. "Hi, Joan. How are you?" she asked.

"More nervous and jumpy than usual after last night," Joan said.

"Not surprising," Kathy said. "I am a little weirded out myself. Figured I would get home before dark."

"Me too."

There was left over mac and cheese in the fridge. Kathy, with her refined palate, couldn't believe what they were eating, but she was spent, and this was easy. They heated the cheesy mac and some frozen peas in the microwave, poured glasses of milk, and plopped down in the living room to eat. Joan shared her thoughts about Sarah and her baby, Anna. Kathy supported Joan's concern and agreed things needed to be monitored carefully.

She also brought up her tunnel terror. "I'm embarrassed about being spooked by this guy in the tunnel. I haven't told anyone but you."

"Sounds like you are being careful given the current circumstances," responded Kathy. "Walking with someone in the tunnel is not a bad idea. Have you heard anything about the body from last night?"

"No. Nothing in the news. Jay didn't say anything about it at lunch. His cousin is a Chicago cop."

"I didn't know that."

"Yes, I've never met him, but it's somehow comforting to know that Jay has a connection with the police."

"That makes sense. It's time for me to call it quits for today."

"Me too. See you in the morning."

Joan climbed into bed and called her mother.

"Hi, Mom. So the tunnel did prove to be daunting."

"How so?"

She reported the incident.

"Joanie, you have to be careful! Make sure you always walk with someone."

"Will try. Not always possible."

She had decided not to discuss the body then. Her mom seemed worried enough with the tunnel episode. She told her how exciting and uplifting the two deliveries were the previous day. She elaborated on her wonderment at watching and possibly assisting a new life enter the world.

Liz responded, "Aunt Eleanor went to Paris to learn obstetrics. At that time, Paris was thought to be the best place in the world to study medicine. The premiere location in Paris for obstetrics was La Maternité. She was not allowed to train there as a doctor because she was a woman. However, it was an institution where young girls trained as midwives, so she entered in that capacity. This was yet another obstacle she succeeded in overcoming to learn her profession. I read her journal entry from September 1849, which states she could witness three thousand deliveries in three months there. She stayed for six."

"Amazing! I saw one yesterday and two the day before, and I thought I was fortunate."

"I am sure you were. You can learn something from each one."

"You're right. One delivery was by C-section and the other two vaginal. I heard lectures about each afterward and read some at the library as well. It's a fascinating field!"

"I am sure it is. How's Jay?"

"Fine. We spent some time together yesterday. He's a little possessive, but I do like him a lot."

As soon as she replaced the receiver, the phone rang again.

"Hi, Joan. It's Jay. I just got out of surgery and another case came in through the ER, so I'm tied up for the night. And I am beat."

"Well, get some sleep when you can."

"Will do. 'Night."

ELEVEN

EASTERN BLUEBIRD: *Sialia sialis*

The only blue bird with a red breast, usually found in small groups in fields or open woods.

March 1980, Chicago, Illinois
1850, London, England

JOAN FELL FAST ASLEEP as soon as she put the receiver down, and there was Aunt Eleanor!

"Aunt Eleanor! What are you doing here?"
"We're going to London."
"Really! You know, I was so shocked to realize that you had a car the last time we met that I didn't look at it. What kind of car is this with its spiffy hunter green body and tan leather seats?"
"I overshot."
"You overshot?"
"I was aiming for 1980 to meet with you and I ended up in 2020, where I saw these great electric cars, Teslas. I bought one and asked if they would add a special BMU button, and they did.
"BMU button?"

"Beam Me Up. I just came from La Maternité in Paris, and we're going to London."

"Again, we defy physics! Why London?"

"We're going to help John Snow with the cholera epidemic. It was raging in London when my family left for America in 1832. Being on the boat for the transatlantic crossing was a great adventure. But then several people on our boat contracted cholera and died. We watched their bodies being dumped into the sea. At age nine, I was old enough to understand and had long-lasting nightmares.

"It is again on the rise now in 1850. John practices obstetrics, but he is a consummate physician in many ways. He had believed that cholera was caused by contaminated water during the first two epidemics in London. This time, he carefully studied the location of the cases. There was a great density near the Broad Street pump, a water source for the local community. In fact, there were five hundred fatal attacks in ten days. All who died were people who lived within two hundred and fifty yards of the pump. We are going to help him dismantle the pump so it can no longer produce water for the community."

"How are we going to manage this?"

"I have a wrench in the trunk," Aunt Eleanor said as they bumped over the cobblestones. She parked her car on Broad Street with a final thump. "I'll pop the trunk. Please get the wrench for me."

Looking around, Eleanor appeared somewhat dismayed. "I don't see John, so I guess we'll just proceed and remove the handle ourselves."

As they walked toward the pump, the aroma of horse droppings on the street in 1850 smacked Joan in the face. Reeling, she concluded that the level of sanitation a century and a half ago clearly left something to be desired. She was jolted out of her reverie when Aunt Eleanor took the wrench from her and, with a flick of her wrist, the pump handle disengaged. She handed it to Joan.

"We'll take this with us. I don't want anyone fixing the pump."

Joan looked in shocked disbelief at the cold, heavy handle in her hand as they walked back to the car. Again, physics was defied. These nights with Aunt Eleanor really were something else. They placed both tools in the trunk, and off they went.

Joan recognized the cold wet tongue on her cheek. Rusty was anxious for his needs to be taken care of.

"Okay, Rusty, give me a minute." *Good grief! I have spent another night with Aunt Eleanor!*

She pulled herself out of bed, showered, and dressed. Turning to her dog, she said, "Okay, let's get you outside."

While walking with Rusty, Joan contemplated her dream. *Mom told me about John Snow just yesterday. Who knew that last night I would play a part in controlling the London cholera epidemic in the 1850s? Kathy's gonna think I am crazy when I tell her about this one.*

Kathy was in the kitchen creating some concoction when Joan and Rusty returned to the apartment, and she looked in disbelief as Joan started to recount her dream. "Joan, when I agreed to room with you, I thought you were a rock-solid, dyed-in-the-wool New Englander. Now I am not so sure," she teased.

Joan shot her a bemused glance as she waved while leaving the apartment. "See you tonight."

Joan made her way to the hospital, noting a pair of eastern bluebirds flitting among the branches of an oak tree along the path. *Those guys are really spectacular. It's such a treat to see them.* She arrived at the hospital and took the stairs to the second floor and her locker.

Having completed the clothing exchange, she descended the three flights to the tunnel. *Oh, man! I'm sweating already, but I told Sarah I would visit first thing in the morning.* As she opened the door, she noted Ernie at the top of the stairway behind her.

"I forgot my stethoscope," he said. "I have to go back. I'll walk with you."

"Great!" she said as she waited for him to descend. "Have you seen Sarah today?" she asked, relieved to be walking with him.

"No, I'll visit later, before her discharge. I want to make sure she has the social work consult."

"Thank you for that. It makes me feel better. I'm going to visit her now." Having passed through the tunnel, they entered the stairwell in the women's hospital and climbed to the fourth floor. Joan proceeded to Sarah's room while Ernie went in search of his stethoscope.

"Hi, Sarah, how are you?"

"Not so well. I have to leave today."

"Has social work come by?"

"Not yet."

"I just saw Dr. Smith. You should see them before you leave. Be sure to tell them about your concerns. How is Anna doing under the bili lights?"

"They say well but probably two more days. It will be April by the time we go home!"

"That's not long."

"It is if I am not here with her," Sarah ruminated. "I'm going to get her now for her feeding."

"Okay. Dr. Smith will be coming by before you are discharged."

Oh dear. She's really worried, but I don't know what else we can do right now. As Joan walked toward the lecture hall, she stopped at a wall phone to page Jay to confirm their luncheon date. She had her OB text, which she read while waiting for his callback. It came, and they agreed on twelve thirty as usual. The lectures were on malignancies of the female genital system, which she found less engaging than the OB talks from yesterday—certainly less uplifting. *OB-GYN is certainly not all new baby and happy family.* As she exited the hall, she saw Jay walking toward her.

"Hi. I had a consult on the OB floor, which doesn't happen very often, so I thought I would meet you so we could walk back together."

"Great idea!" she said while breathing many internal sighs of relief. *Company in the tunnel.*

"How was your morning?"

"Okay. Sarah is really worried about leaving before Anna. She is concerned about somebody taking her baby. I tried to reassure her, but I have my own misgivings after the Baby Jennings incident. Sarah's being discharged today. I spoke to Ernie about her concerns, so he is going to consult social work. I don't know what else to do."

"It sounds like you've got it covered."

"I hope so."

Arriving at the basement tunnel entrance, Jay opened the door and Joan peered through, looking in both directions.

"It's not like we are crossing a street," Jay said, puzzled.

Joan looked back at him. "No, you're right. I was just checking the tunnel."

"For . . . rats?" he quizzed.

"No." She advanced in but was clearly cautious.

"What's going on?"

Joan recounted her tunnel experiences and then her fears.

He looked at her with disbelief. "This has been a challenging time with Baby Jennings's disappearance and the body in the lagoon, but let's not get carried away. You're fine. People walk in the tunnel, lots of people."

I knew I shouldn't tell him. Now what does he think of me? "Well, I'm glad to be walking with you," she said.

He softened and looked down at her. "And ... I'm certainly glad to be walking with you." Checking the empty tunnel in both directions, he leaned down and kissed her on the lips. Her body was stiff with tension. "I'm right here with you. There is nothing to worry about," he said.

That was reassuring, but she was eager to exit the tunnel nonetheless, and she visibly relaxed when they arrived at the basement of the main hospital. They took the elevator up to the cafeteria on the eleventh floor. As the door opened, they were hit with a blast of beef grilling. It smelled good but overwhelming. Their selection was a chicken and cranberry sandwich and a Coke for each.

When seated, she recounted her dream of Aunt Eleanor and the Broad Street pump. She commented on the stench of the streets of London a century ago and explained how she and her aunt had removed the handle and thus helped with the cholera epidemic in London in the 1850s.

"You've had an exciting twenty-four hours. What an intense life you live!"

She looked at him scornfully. "Okay. Now you are either teasing me or making fun of me, or perhaps both.

He took her two hands in his. "Or ... maybe, I'm just happy to be with you," he gently chided.

Their conversation continued amid bites of chicken sandwich, and they left the cafeteria for the afternoon's activities.

"I'll walk you to the library," he said.

"Great! But I haven't heard about your morning."

"It was good. I performed a temporal artery biopsy."

"Temporal artery?"

"The artery that runs right through here," he said putting his fingers on his own temple. "This patient had pain over her right temple and difficulty opening her jaw especially on the right side. It's called giant cell arteritis and can lead to blindness. The diagnosis is made from a biopsy of the artery, and it is treated with steroids. If you diagnose it early enough, you can prevent the subsequent blindness. The procedure went well, and we are waiting for the pathology, but we started the steroids."

"It must be gratifying to be able to make such a difference for your patient."

"It is. I told you ophthalmology was the greatest!" he said, grinning in triumph.

She turned and gave him a "now you're full of yourself" look.

He smiled back at her as she walked through the library door.

Joan reviewed her reading for the morning's lectures and perused a couple of articles suggested by the lecturer. When her thoughts wandered to the woman's body in the lagoon, she decided it was time to go home. She stopped by her locker and promptly made her way outside. As she walked, she mulled over Ernie's reaction to Sarah's concern for her baby and Jay's response to her own concerns about the tunnel.

Guys just don't get it. I guess if you are six foot three and athletic like Jay, you don't feel anxious about people threatening you, because they don't. I had to tell him because I wanted him to understand where I was coming from. I'm not sure we got there.

She arrived at her apartment and ran up the stairs to the tune of Rusty barking. Kathy was home as well.

"How goes it?"

"It goes," Joan responded as she flopped down on the living room couch.

Kathy joined her on an adjacent chair.

"I am still agonizing about specialties," Joan said.

"You're not alone. The whole class is trying to figure this out."

"I am enjoying OB, but I really like being around children."

"I agree with you about spending my day with kids, but I am thinking about pediatric surgery. I like using my hands and solving people's problems with them. I'm rotating off general surgery and taking an elective in pediatric surgery," Kathy said.

"I have been enjoying OB as well."

"Yes, I enjoyed my OB time, and it would be nice to have a female patient population, but that is a really difficult lifestyle. Babies come when they come. On the other hand, I liked the surgical aspects of it. Also, bringing new life into the world is pretty awesome and most often is a joyous time for the parents. To facilitate and share that amazing time has to be rewarding and uplifting."

"I know I don't want to do internal medicine. They spend all day rounding and considering every possible illness in their differential diagnosis whether it's likely or not," Joan said.

"On the other hand, if you chose internal medicine, you could subspecialize in many different areas—cardiology, endocrinology, pulmonology, oncology, the list goes on. Family medicine allows you to follow people for life and develop long-term relationships," Kathy countered.

"I see your point—there are some benefits. However, also in this no-go category for me is psychiatry. I'm not masochistic enough to want to spend my days with angry people directing much of it at me."

"That might not be the most objective view, but I agree with you. On the other hand, psychiatry allows you to deal with the problems of the mind. It can involve literature to the extent that you want it to. Those who chose psych recognize human frailty—including their own, for the most part. The lifestyle is pretty flexible. I know in our psych department, there are some members who are part-time. The men are, for the most part, pretty liberal and less macho than other specialties—surgery, for instance." Kathy thought for a moment. "Of course, Randy is an exception. He's thinking of orthopedics, and he is a really nice guy."

Joan grinned. "Now there's an objective view! I can probably eliminate ortho and general surgery as well. I don't want to be surrounded by colleagues who are pompous cowboy types who think they can do no wrong. I know that does not categorize all surgeons, but there is a stereotype."

"At least they are doers and not just cogitators," Kathy observed.

"Yes, I'll give you that."

"The pediatric surgeons, however, fall less into that stereotypical category."

"You're right. I won't object if you want to become a pediatric surgeon," Joan said with a wink.

"What about you?"

"I am still at the elimination stage. I haven't done any selecting yet, but I'm getting there. I do like pediatrics. Aunt Eleanor and her sister founded the New York Infirmary for Women and Children, so she did some OB."

"I forgot. The police came by," Kathy said.

"The police?"

"Yes. Evidently, they had some more questions about the woman's body. I told them you would be home in an hour or so."

There was a firm knock on the door.

"Just a minute," Joan said. "I'll be right there."

She looked through the peephole in the door and saw two Chicago policemen. They must have been six foot four each and built as well.

Why are these cops always so big? She opened the door.

"Good evening," the first officer said as they both showed their badges.

"Come in," Joan said and led them into the living room. "Would you like some tea?"

"No, thanks. We just have a few questions. After we talked, when we were back at the station, we learned that you had been interviewed recently by our office about a baby. It seems you were the first one to notice that the baby was missing from the nursery."

"That's right. Baby Girl Jennings was one of my assigned babies, and I couldn't find her in the nursery, so I reported this to the head nurse. After unsuccessfully searching further for the baby, she called a Code Pink."

"Also, you were the first to report the body of a woman in the lagoon."

"That's right. I was running with my dog, and we saw the body, and I came home and reported it."

"You seem to be in the middle of things."

Joan shivered at this comment. "What do you mean?" she asked.

"Just that. You seem to be in the middle of things, crimes in particular."

"I report things that I think need reporting, if that's what you mean."

"So do you think there is any connection between these two crimes?"

"I hadn't thought about it. Do you?"

"In fact, we do. The woman in the lagoon was Baby Jennings's mother. You had met her. Didn't you recognize her?"

"Oh my God!" Joan was stunned. Her heart was pounding. Her palms were dripping wet.

She stammered, "Yes. I had met her. No, I did not recognize her. She was somewhat bloated, and I didn't look carefully. It was getting dark, and I was scared and ran home to report it as fast as I could. That's horrific!" She sobbed and then paused. "Just what are you getting at?"

"Nothing. Just trying to review what we know. Thank you for your help. Oh, and please don't leave the city until we get this cleared up."

"What do you mean?"

"Just that. Please don't leave the city until we get this cleared up." They both got up and walked toward the door. "Good night."

TWELVE

MALLARD: *Anas platyrhynchos*

The largest dabbling duck, found in any wet habitat from city parks to tundra ponds. The male has a green iridescent head with a white neck ring and a ruddy breast.

March 1980, Chicago, Illinois
1849, Paris, France

JOAN WAS SHATTERED. She felt like she was falling apart, like a mirror dropped on a marble floor. Suddenly, there were twenty-seven mirrors, all distorted, none as good as the first when they were whole. She sank into the soft overstuffed chair in their living room, totally crushed.

Kathy came in from the kitchen, kneeled on the floor next to the chair, and put her arm around Joan's shoulders. "I heard," she said.

"It sounds like they are accusing me of murder and child abduction," Joan sobbed between huge gasps of air. "What have I done? I didn't do anything except try to be a responsible person."

"I know. I know. Let's review this step-by-step. You were assigned to Baby Jennings. You saw her in the morning but could not find her in the afternoon. You reported her as missing. A Code Pink ensued.

That was back in January before Martin Luther King weekend when you went to visit your mom instead of Bill. Then in March, at the beginning of your OB rotation, you went for a run with Rusty. You saw a woman's body in the lagoon. Now it turns out that the body belongs to the mother of the baby. Ghastly!"

"Denise," Joan said. "Her name is Denise Jennings. I met her just once on my first day in peds. Her brother, Ricky, was in the room with her. He was decidedly creepy. He didn't look at me, and he skulked around the room. When he sat, he sort of slumped in the chair with his hands folded in his lap, his bottom on the edge of the chair, and his knees sticking out. This whole scenario is horrific, and somehow, according to the cops, I am in the middle of it. And . . . through no fault of my own, it appears I *am* in the middle of it."

Joan continued. "Erin mentioned that the child protective team thought there was a ring of baby dealers who preyed on women without resources, offering to buy their babies. The dealers then reneged on the contracts. Looking back on it, we thought Denise had decided to keep her baby because they both had left the hospital. This series of events fits the police hypothesis. Now it seems that the consequences for Denise of keeping her baby included being murdered."

The phone rang, and Kathy went to get it. "It's Jay. He's leaving the hospital and coming here."

"That sounds wonderful! Forget my doubts about Jay. I've got bigger problems!"

"I ordered Chinese, moo shu pork and cashew chicken. There will be plenty for Jay as well. I'm going out to pick it up."

As Kathy headed down the stairs, Jay was coming up. Rusty, hearing feet on the stairway, began to bark.

Jay took the steps two at a time and burst in the door. "What's going on? Kath said something was up."

When he saw her crumpled in the chair, he went over and sat on the arm of the chair and hugged her.

"It looks like I'm a murder suspect and a child abduction suspect," she sobbed.

"What! Wait a minute. Let's just calm down and talk about this."

Joan relayed the evening's events with the police interrogation.

"I'm sure you aren't really a suspect, but they have to conduct their investigation."

"B-but, b-but," she said with faltering breaths.

"I understand you're upset, and you should be, but let's think this through. The police have no recourse but to gather all the information about these two crimes. To your credit, you have been pivotal by initially reporting them, and there it ends. They are just getting started and need to gather all the facts that they can, and you provided the initial facts in both cases."

Kathy entered with the Chinese takeout. "I have food!" she declared, trying to lighten the atmosphere.

"Let's try to calm down and have dinner," Jay said, looking at Joan and squeezing her shoulder. "I'm going to get a beer from the fridge. Anyone else?"

"I'll take one," Kathy said.

"Me too," Joan said resignedly.

"Okay. Three beers for the crowd!" he declared upon returning to the living room.

Kathy brought plates for all. Chopsticks came with the order. The three of them sat around the recycled wire wheel coffee table eating heartily, even Joan.

"Feeling better? The world is always a better place on a full stomach," said Jay.

"I am," Joan acknowledged.

"We'll just see how this plays out. I think I mentioned that my cousin, Dick, is a Chicago cop. He's actually a homicide detective. You may have met two of the guys on his team. I can contact him if things seem to be going in the wrong direction, but I think we just lay low for now. Okay?" he asked Joan.

"You're right, of course. It just was a disturbing interaction with the police. Knowing your cousin is a detective does provide some level of comfort. Thanks," she said, still a little shaky.

"For dessert, we have vanilla ice cream with chocolate sauce!" Kathy announced with a flourish.

They all enthusiastically agreed to take on the ice cream calories.

Following dinner, they stayed in the living room reviewing the police visit and the preceding crimes that had prompted it. Talking about these disturbing events seemed to lessen Joan's panic response and allowed for a more rational discussion of what had occurred. Her friends' support lightened her burden, and her adrenalin level tapered off. All three began to share contagious yawns and realized they were completely beat.

Jay turned to Joan. "I'd like to stay with you tonight if that would be helpful."

"That would be more than helpful," she murmured.

Kathy waved them off. "To bed with you. I command it," she declared.

"We graciously obey," Jay said with a slight bow as they went to Joan's bedroom.

Morning came way too early, but once awake, Joan was eager to get to the hospital and check on Anna, who had spent her first night in the hospital without her mother. She and Jay showered and dressed quickly and were in the kitchen preparing breakfast when Kathy entered.

"I've actually already walked Rusty. He was scratching at your door when you two were showering. I have to get to my lecture, so I'll see you tonight."

Breakfast was just that—fast. Coats on, they left together for the hospital. On the way there, about a block from the lagoon, Joan spotted a male mallard splashing through the lagoon after his mate, who was winning the chase.

"Further evidence that spring is on its way," she said.

They reached the main hospital, and Jay said, "I have to go check on that OB patient I saw yesterday, so I'll walk with you through the tunnel."

She looked up at him. "Terrific!"

The tunnel was navigated without incident, and once on the floor, they went their separate ways.

Joan was smiling at Anna, who was quietly sleeping beneath the bili lights, when Sarah walked up. "She looks good," Joan said. "Less yellow every day."

"Yes. The doctor said she can probably go home the day after tomorrow."

"Did you talk with social work?"

"Yes," Sarah said hesitantly, "but I don't know what they can do."

"Well, just better to have everyone alerted. Are you able to stay for the whole day?"

"Yes. I'll be here."

"Good. See you later."

Joan went off to her morning lectures. Jay paged her and told her he would be in the OR so could not meet for lunch.

She had some trouble focusing on the lectures because the police visit continued to pop into her thoughts and disrupt the topics of ovarian cysts and ectopic pregnancy. She kept picturing them sitting in her living room, questioning. Just thinking about it made her palms sweat. She stayed until the lectures concluded nonetheless and was then off to the cafeteria for a quick yogurt and soup lunch. She followed this with a trip to the library to read and review the morning's lecture topics. Her brain had not taken much in, and she wanted to reinforce what she had heard.

That mission accomplished, she left for home. It was a bright and sunny day, though a little cold.

I'll see about taking Rusty for a run while it is still light.

There was the usual excited greeting from him when she reached the apartment.

After changing into her running gear, she leashed him and said, "Okay, boy. Want to go for a run?"

He was already prancing about in response to being leashed, but now, these were words that he recognized, and he literally jumped for joy.

"Okay, okay. We're going."

They took off in the direction of the lagoon. *I am going to overcome my fear. I am not going to deprive myself of the joy of running by this lagoon.* She trembled a little as they ran by the spot where Denise's body had been but kept going and achieved that milestone. Further on, she spotted another pair of mallards and a blue-winged teal.

So glad I am doing this. Not going to let someone's horrific deed take away my enjoyment of spring. They circled the lagoon and headed for home. "We made it, Rusty!"

After showering, she called her mother. She had already told her about the tunnel. Now she spoke of Denise's body and the connection with Baby Jennings.

"My goodness!" Liz said. "This whole scenario sounds horrific! Are the police on it?"

"Yes. It certainly is a ghastly situation, and evidently, I am a . . . well, no, but they have been by twice to question me."

"What do you mean? Are you saying you are a suspect?"

"No. I talked to Jay about this. His cousin is a homicide detective in Chicago. I just reported both incidents, so they are gathering information for the cases. I had no idea they were linked."

"This has that crawly skin–type scary feel. I am going to talk to your uncle John."

"That sounds good. He may be helpful. Uncle John always knows."

"Joan, be cautious about all of this. You shouldn't be out after dark by yourself. You need to be more careful of that tunnel business. My God, what a mess! More than that, what a horrible series of happenings!"

"I know. I am taking things one at a time and being careful. I have good friends here, so that helps."

"Joan, should I come out?"

"No, Mom. What are you going to do? I promise to be careful, and the police really are on it. I have to proceed with my education. I am not going to let some evil events interfere with that. I'll be fine."

"Okay, but keep me updated."

"I will. I am enjoying OB."

"Well, that's good. I told you about La Maternité."

"You did."

"Okay, love you. Be careful."

"Will do. Love you too."

Emotionally exhausted, Joan went to bed early that night.

Just as she fell asleep, the blurry image of a car hovered on the edge of her mind.

"Aunt Eleanor! What's going on now?"

"I am taking you to La Maternité. I want to show you how things are there. I know you are enjoying obstetrics." They were in her aunt's Tesla with its BMU button. And then... they were at La Maternité in Paris, and the year was 1849. "I think your mother told you that I was not able to come here to learn as a physician because they didn't allow women—just men—for that training. My desire to become an accomplished obstetrician was not to be thwarted, so I had to devise another approach. I enrolled as a midwife."

They walked through a large gate in a high wall that surrounded many buildings encircling a courtyard.

Entering the building nearest the gate, Eleanor said, "We're not allowed to leave La Maternité during our training, so I am locked in here for six months." She winked. "But I have a way around that, as you know. Here's where I sleep. Fifteen of us share this room, and we have no sleep three to four nights a week delivering babies. Here is the bathing room." Joan looked at the six tubs lined up in a single room. "We can take baths from two to three in the afternoon after lectures. I sink down in the water, close my eyes, and pretend I am alone."

"I can understand that," Joan said. The overriding theme was a total lack of privacy.

"Let's go to the labor and delivery ward," Eleanor said.

There were two beds occupied of the eight that were there. Joan noticed the wet mattresses of the unoccupied beds from previous deliveries. Students were bringing clean linens and making up the beds, but the mattresses emitted a foul odor. She observed one vaginal delivery and compared it to her previous experience. Hands were not washed; there were no gloves, no sterile preparation. The mothers were screaming in agony intermittently with contractions. There was no anesthesia, no epidural. How different from her experience in 1980 in Chicago on so many levels, different in the living situation for the trainees, different in the level of hygiene, different in the practice of medicine, and a very different experience for the patients.

After the birth, Eleanor took Joan's elbow and said, "Time to go." She ushered her to the car, and with the push of a button, Joan was back in Chicago and the year was 1980.

THIRTEEN

DOWNY WOODPECKER: *Picoides pubescens*
Our smallest woodpecker, these birds sport a distinctive white, black, and red cap.

April 1980, Chicago, Illinois

A RAY OF EARLY APRIL sunlight snuck through the not quite closed shade in Joan's east-facing window and beamed its way to her sleeping right eye. She squeezed her lid then blinked and sat bolt upright.

"Sarah and Anna! I have been thinking all this time about Denise and her baby, and then about me and my being a suspect. But... they may be at risk. I have to talk to Sarah this morning." With that, she was up, in the shower, dressed, and on her way to the kitchen for a quick breakfast.

Kathy was there. "I took Rusty along for my morning run, so you don't have to walk him."

"Great! Thanks, Kath. I'm going to go over to see my patient Sarah. She's the one with Baby Anna who is under the bili lights. She's been worried about her baby being taken from the hospital. I hope she is not caught up in this baby-for-pay ring. I have to warn her."

"Wait. Think about this. How are you going to present it to her? You can't just walk in and talk to her as if she has sold her baby. You don't want to add to her fears if she hasn't."

"I know. You're right. It is a delicate situation, but I feel that I have to do something."

"I'll grant you that. What did the social work consult say?"

"They just made sure Sarah had transportation to and from the hospital covered after she was discharged so she can visit Anna while she is under the bili lights. They also checked the living situation and childcare availability for when she returns to her waitressing job. She has a sister with a baby, and they will be sharing childcare duties with some supplement from the outside. Nothing more than that in the consult."

"Just be cautious. You don't want to make the situation worse. Also, remember that you might be a suspect. Be careful about placing yourself in the middle of it again."

"I know, but I have to do something. I would never forgive myself if the situation with Baby Jennings and Denise repeated itself. I'll just try to gently introduce the topic and see where it goes."

Joan made her way to the hospital and then to the tunnel. She stuck her head into the entrance from the basement of the main hospital. It smelled dank and sour as she looked left and right. She was going right. To the left, she saw a shadowy figure moving away across the cold, dirty gray tiles. She shivered uncontrollably. *Good grief. This place is so creepy!*

She waited until the figure turned a corner far to the left and then entered to the right, walking quickly but as quietly as she could on the hard tiles. She arrived at the basement entrance to the women's hospital and took the stairs to the fourth floor.

In the newborn nursery, she saw Anna under the bili lights looking less yellow. *Great, she's responding well.*

At that point, Sarah entered the nursery.

"She looks even better," said Joan.

"Yes, she does. They think I can take her home tomorrow. They're going to check the bilirubin again in the morning, but it's going in the right direction."

"Sarah, can we go into the consultation room and talk for a minute?"

Sarah looked concerned. "Anything wrong? We haven't done this before."

"No. I just want to touch base on something now that you are getting close to going home."

"Aren't I gonna to see you tomorrow?"

"Of course you are, but I just want to talk for a minute today."

Sarah agreed, and they walked to the consultation room together. Once in and seated, Joan began. "Sarah, before you gave birth to Anna, there was an incident with a baby disappearing from the interim nursery in the main hospital."

Sarah gasped.

"Wait. Here me out. She was not under the lights, not in the women's hospital nursery where Anna is. Have you heard of being able to earn money by giving birth to a baby and selling it?"

Sarah looked at her with a face filled with fear. She hesitated and was tremulous.

"Are you all right?" Joan asked with concern.

"Yes. I have to tell you this. I can't let them go on stealing babies," she said, obviously distressed. "They contacted my sister, Jill, about her daughter, Sasha, before she was born."

"After she was pregnant but before the birth? How did they find her?"

"Yes, when she was pregnant. She had a friend who had lost her job, couldn't pay for rent or food, and was really desperate. She didn't want to live on the street, so she contracted to provide a baby. They paid her some in advance to tide her over. She borrowed some money from Jill and succeeded in getting a housecleaning job while she was pregnant. She still has the job, and she paid Jill back, but they never came through with the final payment for the baby. A guy visited her in the hospital after delivery and claimed he was her brother so he was a known, accepted visitor. The next night, he stole the baby from the nursery. She didn't report anything because she was afraid of the consequences for herself, and she wasn't planning on keeping the baby. She just discharged herself from the hospital. Jill would have nothing to do with them when they contacted her."

"What about you?"

"I refused, just like Jill. But these evil guys are around, and I am afraid of losing Anna."

"What about when you go home? Are you afraid they will come and take her?"

"It seems that it is easier for them in the hospital. They dress in hospital scrubs and take the babies during the night shift and disappear into the tunnel system. They want newborns because they can get a higher price. But you're right. We do have to be careful at home too."

Joan tried to reassure her, but neither of them felt comfortable. "Thank you for telling me. We have to find a way to stop this."

"I am just going to stay in the hospital with Anna tonight," Sarah said. "No one is going to take my baby!"

"I will try to make sure that doesn't happen either."

"What are you gonna do?" asked Sarah, wide-eyed.

"The police have been questioning me about the other baby because I was the one who first reported her missing."

"The police!" exclaimed Sarah.

"You and your sister have done nothing wrong, and now you have two babies to protect. The police are the only ones who can get to the bottom of this. We can't let it go on."

"But . . . I suppose you are right."

"Let's go back to the nursery, and you stay with Anna as you had planned. I will go and check on all of this. Here's my pager number, and here is my home phone number."

Sarah looked at her with some trepidation, clearly unsettled, as they walked to the nursery. There was Anna sleeping peacefully under her bili lights with the mask over her eyes to protect them from the lights. Sarah settled in, and Joan went to the nursing station. She was surprised to find Jackie, the head nurse with whom she reviewed the abduction of Baby Girl Jennings. Evidently, she had been the charge nurse in the interim nursery until this upgraded nursery was opened in the women's hospital and now was in charge here.

Joan expressed her concern about Anna. She told Jackie that Sarah was going to stay with Anna until she was discharged.

The nurse agreed and paged Ernie for Joan.

"Hi, Ernie. Can you meet me in the break room?"

"Sure. I just finished a delivery and was going there myself to dictate the report."

Joan thanked the nurse and walked to the break room where Ernie sat dictating. Fortunately, they were alone.

"What's up?" he asked.

She recounted the Baby Jennings story, including the death of her mother, of which he was not aware. "This all has to remain confidential," she warned.

He agreed, and she went on about her conversation with Sarah and both their concerns about Anna.

He whistled. "Boy, you are an exciting medical student to work with!"

She winced. "Don't say that! I have been hearing it too much lately. I don't need an exciting life. I just need a life. Anyway, I wanted you to be aware."

"I can call in protective services and security and let them know about a worrisome uncle."

"Please, let Sarah know first. I just don't want her to totally freak out."

"Will do."

As Joan was walking toward the stairway, she ran into Jay.

"Hi, I just finished my follow-up on my OB patient. Want to walk to lunch together?" he asked.

"There's no one I would rather walk with through the tunnel," she said, putting her arm through his.

"What's up?" he asked as they descended the stairs to the basement.

She recounted the conversation with Sarah.

"Does Ernie know?"

"I talked to Ernie, and he is calling in the protective services team and notifying security."

They reached the tunnel. Joan looked in and, while recoiling from the damp air, checked in both directions.

He smiled and said, "I understand, and you are right on target. We all have to be careful in this tunnel."

"Good! Glad you agree."

When they reached the cafeteria and had obtained their turkey and brie sandwich fare, they found *their* table near the window.

"What do you think I should do about the police?" asked Joan.

"Tell them about Sarah and Anna. You want them to investigate and protect Sarah and her baby and possible future victims, and you have information that will help."

"But I may be a suspect, and this puts me in the middle again."

"Granted, but you are already there, and you can help. How about if I call my cousin Dick and speak to him off the record?"

"That sounds good."

"I'll try to get to him today."

"Great! I'll wait until we touch base before contacting the police."

Their lunch finished, Jay left for the ophthalmology clinic and Joan headed to the library, having missed the morning lecture. The afternoon flew by in the midst of her readings about postpartum infections and infections of the newborn. She left the hospital well before dark and walked home, enjoying the smells of spring. The magnolias and weeping cherry trees were blossoming, and the daffodil bulbs were flowering.

She heard and saw a downy woodpecker *tap, tap, tapping* to get at some bugs in the bark. "Get those guys," she encouraged.

She reached their apartment and was greeted by Rusty's hello. "Hi, Rust. We'll go for a nice walk on this beautiful spring day." As always, he was eager and excited when he heard the word *walk*. She leashed him, and they descended the stairs with him in the lead. "We're going by the lagoon," she told him.

To herself, she again vowed not to avoid this lovely spot because of someone else's evil doings. The sun washed over her skin, and the scent of early lilacs filled the air. Another downy woodpecker was *rat-tat-tatting* overhead.

I'm back!

They rounded the lagoon and were on their way home when they spotted Jay heading toward Joan's apartment. "Hey, hello there."

He turned and waved. "Hi. Just coming to see you." They met at the corner. "I talked to my cousin Dick. He said, as we thought, you should report the information you have to help their investigation. He confirmed that you are not necessarily a suspect. I know you'll still be worried about that, as I would be."

"I'm freaked out about that, but I think it is best to talk to them as well." The three climbed the steps to Joan's apartment. "Kathy and I have spaghetti in the fridge that we made last night, and I can make a salad as well. Do you want to stay for dinner?"

"Love to. Our fridge is empty except for beer."

As Joan walked toward the refrigerator, there was a loud knock on the door. "I've heard that knock before," she said as she cast an anxious glance toward Jay.

"The cops?" he mouthed.

Joan nodded yes. She went to the door and opened it.

There stood the same two very tall policemen with their badges in hand.

"We have a few more questions," said the slightly taller one, who was maybe six foot five.

"Come in," said Joan. She walked before them into the living room. "This is my friend Jay."

There was a shaking of hands all around, and then everyone sat down.

The taller policeman began. "Did you know Denise before you met her in the maternity ward?"

"No."

"Are you sure?"

Joan gave him a withering look. "Yes."

"Do you know what her occupation is?"

"No. Should I know? I'm not sure how that is relevant."

Jay cast her a "just go along with this" glance.

The policeman went on. "We think her murder may have something to do with her baby disappearing from the nursery. What do you think?"

"I think so too. As a matter of fact, I was going to call you, but you beat me to the punch. I'm concerned about another baby who's now in the nursery—and her mother." Joan went on to tell them of Sarah and Anna and what Sarah had told her about the baby-for-pay ring.

The police listened without comment.

She continued. "Sarah is spending the night in the nursery with Anna, who's supposed to be discharged tomorrow. I think there should be a police presence with them until they go home. You could also go and talk with Sarah yourselves. As I said, her sister was approached by the ring but refused. They may both be at risk even if they didn't sign a contract."

"That's not a bad idea. We can swing by the hospital on our way out. Thank you for the information. It may prove to be helpful, but our previous order still holds. Don't leave the city until things are cleared up."

As she ushered them out, Joan said, "You know this sounds like a complicated ring. It may not be cleared up for quite a while."

They both turned and looked back at her with raised eyebrows and descended the stairs.

FOURTEEN

YELLOW-BELLIED SAPSUCKER: *Sphyrapicus varius*
One of a species of long-winged, delicate woodpeckers with yellow breasts. They drill horizontal rows of shallow holes in tree bark from which they drink sap and eat insects.

April 1980, Chicago, Illinois

JOAN RETURNED TO the living room, sighing, and Jay hugged her.

"Good job, Joanie. Your interaction with the police was spot-on. Hopefully, they'll go and watch over Anna and Sarah tonight and move further with their investigation."

She nodded yes while trying to muffle a sob. "Good grief! I am not good at this."

"No one is. The people who deal with these situations have had years of training in order to manage. You have not had years of training."

"I know. You're right." She took a deep breath. "But I feel so accused."

"You're not."

She glanced back at him with a helpless, brow-raised look.

He hugged her and rose to move toward the kitchen. "Are you hungry? Everything is better on a full stomach.

With that, they retrieved the spaghetti from the refrigerator, heated it in the microwave, and assembled a salad. They moved to the living room with their fare and were just beginning to eat when Kathy came in.

"Hi, guys," she greeted. "Looks like dinner. Can I join you?"

"Of course," they chimed in together.

Joan updated Kathy about Anna and Sarah, with Jay adding bits here and there.

When they had recounted the happenings, Kathy responded, "Never a dull moment! It sounds like things are starting to come into hand but clearly still worrisome."

"Yes. I'll go check in with Sarah first thing in the morning," Joan said, finishing her dinner.

Jay, taking his plate to the kitchen, said "I'm going back to my apartment to pick up a few things."

Joan walked with him to the door where he turned to her, gave her a bear hug, and placed a long, wet, pressing kiss on her lips.

She kissed back enthusiastically.

After a quiet moment, he said, "This is all going to be fine. We just have to take it one step at a time, and you are doing very well with that. *And . . .* I'm on your side."

"I know. See you soon?"

"Yes. I'll be back." He turned and headed down the stairs.

Joan returned to the living room.

"How are you?" Kathy asked.

"I'm doing okay. This whole thing is scary and exhausting, but I think I can help with solving it, so that part feels good." They sat in the living room quietly talking about the baby-for-pay ring, and then Kathy turned the conversation to Randy.

"Randy and I have been seeing each other. He is an interesting guy, and there is this attraction thing."

"Attraction thing?" Joan asked.

"There aren't many guys that I could view as more than friends, but he is one of them."

"One of them? Who are the others?"

"There are no others. I just mean theoretically. Anyway, don't give me a hard time," she insisted. "I really like him!"

"Well, that sounds great! As you know, I am feeling closer and closer to Jay as well. Let's set something up that removes us from my current dilemma and medical school in general, and just have some fun. Maybe we can start with tennis."

"Good idea! I'll talk to Randy about it."

"I'm going to call my mom. I told her I would update her."

With that, Joan went to her room. "Hi, Mom."

"Hi, Joanie. How are you? What's up?"

"Just wanted to touch base." She told her about the second visit by the police and Sarah and Anna.

"I hope the police went and watched over Sarah and her baby. Did you say they were to go home tomorrow?" Liz asked.

"Yes. I am going to stop by first thing in the morning. Sarah was going to spend the night with Anna in the nursery. I want to see them before Anna is discharged."

"I spoke to your uncle John about all of this. He felt that you were not really a suspect but just a source of information vital to the case. He said not to worry about the suspect thing, but I know you and I will have angst about this anyway. However, his thoughts are reassuring. On a more upbeat topic, what was your lecture on today?"

"I missed the lectures because I was talking with Sarah. The topics were postpartum infections and infections of the newborn, so I spent much of the afternoon reading up on these topics."

"Maybe not so upbeat, but interesting. I was just reading about puerperal fever in your aunt's journal."

"Puerperal fever?"

"It's another name for postpartum infection. It was used in the eighteen hundreds because they knew of the fever that could afflict mothers in the immediate postpartum period but not the cause. They didn't know it was due to a bacterial infection of the uterus and the genital tract. Anyway, she writes about two doctors who were her contemporaries, Oliver Wendell Holmes of Boston who wrote *The Contagiousness of Puerperal Fever* in 1843, and Ignaz Semmelweis, who lectured on this in 1850 at the Vienna Medical Society. Puerperal fever or childbed fever followed delivery and was associated with abscesses in the abdomen and lungs and pus flowing from the birth canal, and it often resulted in death within twenty-four hours."

"How horrific!"

"Both of them concluded that the disease was spread by practicing obstetricians. As you can imagine, this view was not applauded by the physicians at the time. Semmelweis presented comparative data for midwife births and doctor births. The incidence of puerperal fever was ten to twenty times more frequent in the births that were managed by the physicians. Evidently, they would perform autopsies on women who had died of puerperal fever with their bare hands, not wash them, move on to the next delivery, and inoculate the next mother with the bacteria they had on their hands from the autopsy. There was no understanding of germ theory at that time. The midwives, of course, did not perform autopsies, so the incidence of this disaster was much lower in the mothers delivered by midwives. Semmelweis's mantra was 'Wash your hands!'"

"A good idea in general."

"Yes, it is. Well, I'm an hour ahead of you and falling asleep, so I am going to sign off. Be careful, Joan. Love you."

Joan had already prepared for bed, and when she put her head on the pillow, she immediately fell asleep. The past couple of days had been exhausting in many ways.

Jay came in about an hour later and, seeing her sleeping, snuck into her bed, gave her a soft kiss on her forehead, and succeeded in not wakening her.

When morning arrived, they briefly made up for missing each other the previous night with some hungry kissing, but then they were up and at 'em. Joan was eager to get to the hospital and see Sarah and Anna, and Jay had clinic responsibilities. They breakfasted and did a speed walk with Rusty. Finally on their way, a warm, sunny April day greeted them. Joan pointed out to Jay a yellow-bellied sapsucker climbing a nearby linden tree.

"I am loving this learning about birds. It makes me much more observant when I am outside, even in the city."

"That's what my mom preaches, and this city in particular," responded Joan. "Lake Michigan is a migration route with birds resting at Montrose Harbor, Wooded Isle, and Jackson Park in particular. So you not only see the indigenous birds but the migratory birds as well. It's pretty amazing."

They arrived at the hospital, stopped on the second floor to leave their outside coats and don their inside lab coats, and proceeded down to the tunnel.

"I'll escort you through the tunnel, madam," Jay said with a half bow and a flourish.

"Okay. Now you are teasing me," said Joan as she shoved his shoulder.

They sped through the tunnel and up to the fourth floor, where they separated.

"Good luck with Sarah and Anna," said Jay.

"Thanks. See you," said Joan as she proceeded to the nursery.

There she found Sarah sitting adjacent to a window and breastfeeding Anna with gentle sunlight washing over both of them.

"You two look beautiful and peaceful," Joan said with relief. "Anna continues to look less yellow. It's almost all gone."

"Yes. I didn't sleep much last night." Sarah sighed. "But the good news is that Anna looks better and nothing happened. Well, not nothing. The police arrived and told me they had been talking with you. One of them stayed outside the nursery all night. So that was reassuring."

"Great! That's what I was hoping for."

At this point, the two policemen that Joan had spoken with the previous night entered the nursery, showing their badges to the head nurse. She escorted them over to Sarah and Joan.

"Everything okay?" the taller one asked.

Sarah explained that her hospital stay was uneventful and she appreciated the police guard through the night.

"Just doing our job," they responded. "Are you and the baby being discharged today?"

"I think so. Joan, my medical student, is here, but I haven't seen the attending physician or the resident."

They nodded at Joan.

"Well, we will want to stay in touch. We have your address and phone number. Here are some phone numbers for us, and of course, there is 911. Don't hesitate to call us if anything suspicious happens. We will contact you in the next week for follow-up. Any questions?"

"No. I don't think so. Thank you."

"No problem." With that, they left the nursery.

Joan looked at Sarah. "What do you think?"

"I hope we go home today and that is the end of all this."

"Yes, but this baby-for-pay ring is still out there, so the police probably will be calling on you for any further information you may have. After all, the ring contacted both you and your sister. Also, you may have more friends that they approach in the future."

"I suppose so, but I would like to have this over."

"We all would, but we have to help the police in any way we can to stop these people."

Joan went to the nursing station to let them know she was leaving.

"Dr. Smith should be arriving any minute," the nurse said.

"Would you ask him to page me when he knows if Anna is going to be discharged?"

Joan proceeded to the lecture hall to hear the second half of the infection lectures. They had additional meaning after talking with her mother last night. Just as she was leaving the lecture hall, her pager rang. It was Jay saying he was tied up and couldn't meet for lunch.

She headed to the cafeteria to get her lunch, and her pager rang again. This time it was Ernie, who wanted to let her know that Anna was going to be discharged today.

"Hooray!" said Joan. "Thank you for letting me know. I'm thrilled they'll be going home."

Arriving at the cafeteria, she ran into Kathy.

"Hi, Kath. I never see you here."

"Yeah, I know. I have a break between cases. Do you want to take advantage of this opportunity to have lunch together?"

"Great idea!"

They bought their lunches. The table near the window where Joan and Jay often ate was available, so they snatched it up.

"This is terrific! We never have a chance to do this, a ladies' leisurely lunch," Kathy said with a flick of her wrist.

"Update," said Joan. "Anna is being discharged today!"

"Great! Hopefully the end of that saga, but of course, there's the Jennings mother and baby."

"Yes, but I am breathing a sigh of relief to have Sarah and Anna leave the hospital, making it less likely that scenario will repeat itself."

"Agreed! Let's talk about tennis. I could reserve one of the courts near the pool for Saturday while I am there for my swim tonight. I am going to stop there before coming home."

"Sounds good. Maybe at one o'clock when morning rounds are most likely over. I'll check with Jay this afternoon."

"Okay. So overall, how are you doing with this crime cascade?"

"Better today, but of course not resolved. How are you and Randy doing?"

"Really well. We fit together. We're both sort of jocks. We each want to be surgeons, and we know what that means for lifestyle. He's very bright and really responsible. He's also a sexy guy, and I love being with him. He just lifts my spirits, makes me feel good."

"It sounds like you're all in. Though I had my doubts, I am feeling like that, too, with Jay. He makes me feel safe and comfortable in these crazy times. You haven't heard anything more about his girlfriend from Randy, have you?"

"No, nothing."

"And you will let me know if you hear anything?"

"Of course. How could you even ask?"

Joan shrugged.

They both realized they had to get on with their afternoon responsibilities—Joan in the library and Kathy back in surgery.

Joan reviewed the notes from the infection lectures. The perspective her mother had provided for her piqued her interest, and she explored some other primary articles as well, including some history. Oliver Wendell Holmes's life was particularly compelling. He lived in Boston and was a contemporary of Aunt Eleanor—and Thomas Wentworth Higginson, whom her mother had studied extensively.

For Joan, Aunt Eleanor was larger than life and still a living being. "I wonder if they knew each other?" she mused.

Enthralled, the afternoon passed quickly, and she was on her way home before she knew it.

FIFTEEN

AMERICAN GOLDFINCH: *Carduelis tristis*

The only small yellow bird with black wings. Undulating flight when foraging for weed seeds and tree buds.

April 1980, Chicago, Illinois
1850, Vienna, Austria

JOAN CALLED JAY to set up tennis for the next day, a precious Saturday. He was eager about the prospect and had already received a heads-up from Randy.

As Kathy came in the door, Joan called out that tennis was confirmed by Jay, as well, and she was going to bed early. A lot had been happening in addition to her studies, and it was starting to take its toll.

Falling asleep immediately, she noted Aunt Eleanor's car.

"Aunt Eleanor! Where are we going tonight?"

"To Vienna. This puerperal fever epidemic is completely out of hand. Young mothers are dying at an alarming rate, by the hundreds."

"What about Holmes in Boston? I just read about him."

"He is part of an established New England family and will be fine. We need to help Ignaz Semmelweis. The poor man is being dismissed as a

crank at the Vienna General Hospital because he is Hungarian and Jewish. He may be a little quirky, but his thoughts on puerperal fever are right on, and he needs our support."

"What can we possibly do?"

"Look in the back seat. I have made posters to disseminate."

Joan turned to the back seat and saw stacks of signs that commanded: "Wasche Deine Hände! Wash Your Hands!"

She looked back at her aunt incredulously.

"I know. I have thumbtacks, and we are going to post these throughout the hospital."

As in the past, they were almost immediately at their destination in Aunt Eleanor's Tesla with the BMU button. She parked it and popped open the trunk, which held more stacks of posters. It was late in the evening, and the hospital grounds were quiet.

"You take a pile of my pamphlets, and I will carry the thumbtacks," she instructed Joan.

Then, hall by hall, and floor by floor, they tacked up the posters. They did not skip the restrooms, both the ladies' and the gentlemen's, as there were few people about. When they did run into anyone, they smiled and said they were helping Dr. Semmelweis. Joan was surprised that this explanation seemed to be accepted by the weary workers on the night shift. The two stopped only when the hospital was virtually plastered with posters and their supply ran out.

They rounded a corner on their way to Eleanor's car and almost ran into a tall, thin gentleman with a very bushy mustache. He looked at them and then at one of their signs and gave a thumbs-up as he walked around the corner.

"Oh my!" said Aunt Eleanor. "That's the man himself."

The morning was bright and sunny, about seventy-five degrees, a great day for tennis. Joan wandered into the kitchen, where Kathy was making breakfast.

"Hi, Kath. Do you have to go into the hospital this morning?"

"No. I am going to have a leisurely breakfast," she said smiling broadly.

"Do you want to go for a run with Rusty and me before eating?"

"Love to. Just let me find my running shorts. I haven't had bare legs since last fall."

"I'll need to do that too."

They both searched and then donned their running gear and met in the kitchen again, where Joan leashed Rusty. The three bounced down the stairs, exuding energy.

"What a great morning! I want to go by the lagoon. I'm working on not developing a phobia about our lovely lagoon."

"Sounds good to me." Kathy nodded in agreement.

They had reached the lagoon when Joan noticed a small bright yellow bird flitting through the branches of an adjacent tree. "Kathy, a goldfinch! The first one I've seen this year. How great! Did you see it?"

Kathy, who was not a birder, said, "I did see a yellow bird. What do you know—so that's a goldfinch. You're going to turn me into a birder yet, Joanie."

"Look in that blooming redbud. There's a blue-gray gnatcatcher sitting on the lower right branch. Nope, flew."

"I missed that one."

"They don't sit for long," Joan said.

They ran on, enjoying the warm weather and the beginnings of spring. Rounding the corner of the lagoon, they saw their neighbor Erin running with her dog, Lily.

"Hi, Erin," they both shouted simultaneously. "Any news on Baby Jennings?"

"Nothing new." Erin waved back and was on her way to the lagoon.

The apartment was straight ahead, and the three mounted the stairs a little less energetically than they had descended on their way out. Kathy showered while Joan made peanut butter and jelly sandwiches. They then reversed roles, and Joan showered while Kathy poured milk and set the table. They dressed for tennis in shorts and T-shirts. Whites weren't required on the school courts. Wolfing down their sandwiches, they put on baseball caps and sunglasses, picking up their tennis rackets before making their way down the stairs.

When they arrived at the courts, Jay and Randy were warming up.

"Hi, girls," Jay said. "Randy and I were thinking we would play a set and then maybe we could all play mixed doubles. What do you think?"

"We're fine playing singles. It will be a good warm up for us," said Kathy, who had played more tennis than Joan.

The games commenced, and all four were working up a sweat. The guys' score tied at five games each. They played the next game, and Jay won the set. At that point, the girls were four games each, but they were willing to call it a draw and begin the mixed doubles. Joan joined Jay and Kathy partnered with Randy.

They decided to take a breather after six games, score tied. They gathered under an adjacent umbrella and guzzled some water. Sunglasses were removed to cool their faces in the fountain. Joan, looking at Randy, noted for the first time that his pupils were different sizes. She thought of saying something but decided to wait and discuss this with Jay.

They resumed play. Joan and Jay won the seventh game, making the score four to three. Randy seemed to be missing some of the high lobs. The "J and J team" won the set, and all four returned to the umbrella for more water.

Joan leaned over to Jay and whispered, "Randy's pupils are different sizes."

"What do you mean?"

"Just what I said. I noticed it when he took off his sunglasses under the umbrella."

At that point, Randy said, "I was having trouble with receiving lobs. Not sure what's going on. The ball seems to disappear."

Joan looked at Jay and tilted her head quizzically.

"How long have you noticed this?" Jay asked him.

"Just today for the first time, but I haven't played tennis in months."

"Let me take a look," Jay said. "Take off your sunglasses."

Randy complied.

"Have you noticed that your pupils are different sizes?"

"No, not particularly," Randy replied.

"They are. Joan picked it up, but I'm embarrassed to say, I didn't quite believe her. Shows you what a sap I am."

"I might agree with that," Joan said as she shoved Jay's shoulder.

Jay faced Randy. "Cover each eye separately. Do things look about the same out of each eye individually?"

"I think so," Randy responded.

"Let's try something else. Cover your left eye with your hand, and I am going to hold up some fingers in four quadrants. You continue to look straight ahead. Tell me how many fingers you see."

Randy complied and counted the correct number of fingers everywhere except up.

Jay repeated the process on Randy's left eye, and he had the right count everywhere.

"Hmmm. I think we had better go to the eye clinic," Jay said.

"Now? Are you kidding? It's Saturday."

"Randy, you need to be checked out. Something's not right."

"I just missed a few returns. That's all."

"You need a dilated exam."

"I don't want a dilated exam."

"I understand that."

"Randy," Kathy said, "how about if we all go to the hospital? Joan and I will get a Coke in the cafeteria while you and Jay go to the eye clinic. You can join us for the thirty minutes that it takes for your pupils respond to the drops and dilate."

Randy sent a pained look toward Kathy.

She put her arm through his. "I'll buy some chips too. What kind shall we get?"

"You decide."

"Okay."

The four of them gathered up their tennis gear and moved together toward the hospital. The guys exited the elevator on the fourth floor for the eye clinic, and the girls stayed on until the eleventh floor and the cafeteria.

"What do you think?" Kathy asked Joan.

"I don't know, but his pupils are different sizes. I have been trying to be observant about pupils after seeing three different patients with abnormal pupils on my peds rotation. I don't think Randy's looked like that before."

"What does it mean?"

"I don't know, but Jay will check him out. If he needs help, he will get a fellow or an attending to look at him. We'll soon know something concrete. Let's get some Coke and chips."

They picked out some Lay's potato chips and some Fritos corn chips and sat at the table near the window that Joan had now claimed as their designated table. At first, they sat in silence, sipping Coke and chewing chips, with Kathy looking very worried.

"Joan, what if he is losing his vision? He won't be able to be a surgeon. That could destroy him, my perfect guy . . . so strong." She started to tear up.

"Now, Kath, you know better than that. We should not go down a disaster path unless we absolutely have to. We have no idea what's going on. Neither of us knows enough even to speculate on the possibilities. Let's think positively until we know more."

"Of course you're right, but that's not so easy right now."

"I know. Let's just try to keep it together for Randy's sake."

The guys exited the elevator. Jay immediately knew the most likely table and directed Randy toward the girls.

"So?" asked Joan upon their arrival.

"So Randy's central vision is normal in each eye, and his anterior exam is normal except for the left pupil, which has a small irregularity, probably due to a tear," Jay reported. "I think it may have occurred when we had the car accident and Randy's head hit the steering wheel." The girls looked at each other wincing. "He's had his dilating drops."

"I've had my dilating drops and, already, I don't like it," Randy chimed in.

"Well, here's a Coke and have some chips. We even have choices, potato or corn," encouraged Kathy as she put her arm through his.

With the four of them chatting and eating, the half hour passed quickly, and Jay and Randy were heading back to the eye clinic.

"Why don't you two stay here, and we will come and join you as soon as we are finished. It shouldn't take long," Jay said. "See you in a few."

The girls agreed, and Joan tried to steer the conversation to other topics while they waited for the guys to return. "I had another crazy Aunt Eleanor dream last night. We went to Vienna in her car and helped Ignaz Semmelweis with his campaign against puerperal fever by plastering his hospital with signs encouraging handwashing."

"I am not familiar with Semmelweis at all," Kathy said.

Joan explained further and, as she did so, the guys returned with Randy looking stricken.

"So what's going on?" Joan asked.

"Randy has a retinal detachment."

The girls looked dumbfounded.

Jay went on. "The retina is like the film in a camera, and it has been lifted off the tissues behind it by some fluid. That's why he is having trouble seeing the ball when it comes from above."

Randy shuffled his feet.

"Come sit with us," Kathy encouraged as she reached for his hand.

Jay said, "He'll have a procedure tomorrow. He needs to be still, and it's probably best to keep his head up until then, so he will have to sleep sitting up."

"Great! My favorite position for sleeping!" Randy responded with no small amount of sarcasm.

"Let's go to our place. We can watch movies, play some cards, and veg out. The butcher shop is on the way. How about a couple of steaks and baked potatoes for dinner? The bakery on our street makes great cherry pies," Joan said.

Jay joined in. "You two can go directly to the apartment, and Joan and I will get dinner preparations."

Kathy and Randy said little but nodded in assent as they walked toward the girls' building.

When they were out of earshot, Joan turned to Jay. "So?"

"His retina is detached below, so it is affecting his field above. I think the most likely case scenario is that he got a small retinal tear when he hit his head on the steering wheel during the car accident. Then, over time, fluid leaked through this opening, and he developed a retinal detachment. He may have gotten a small iris tear at the same time. His irises are dark brown, so pupil size is not so obvious. Good spot that you noticed it, Joan!"

She smiled at the compliment. "What about the prognosis?"

"He is still twenty-twenty. Hopefully, the surgery goes well, and he maintains that and recovers some of the peripheral loss."

"Good grief! I hope so."

"Let's just try to make this a relaxed afternoon. One of the retinal attendings is coming in tomorrow morning to operate on him. He is a very good surgeon, so that's Randy's best shot. We'll try to help him relax and have the time pass quickly until then. He will have to be NPO—nothing by mouth—after midnight, so we'll make a great steak dinner for tonight."

He hugged her shoulder as they moved toward the butcher shop.

SIXTEEN

HERMIT THRUSH: *Catharus guttatus*
A brown-backed bird with a slender bill and a spotted breast; larger than a sparrow. The reddish tail is conspicuous as the bird flies away.

May 1980, Chicago, Illinois

IT WAS THE BEGINNING of May. Joan's OB rotation was ending and her pathology section beginning.

Randy had his surgery Sunday morning, and Kathy spent the afternoon and evening with him at the hospital. She walked home just after seven when he was going to go to sleep. When she arrived at their apartment, Joan was sitting in the living room studying.

"Hi, Kath. How's the boy?"

"It was time to head for home. He's sleeping. His general anesthetic hadn't completely worn off, and he was exhausted from the ordeal. Had an eventful couple of days. His surgeon said the procedure went well, so here's hoping," she said with fingers crossed in front of her chest."

"I'll second that! He certainly has had a great deal on his plate. How are you holding up?"

"I'm tired, but other than that, okay."

"Have you eaten?"

"No. Let's just have pizza delivered. I don't want to have to do anything."

"Agreed."

The girls lounged and reviewed the weekend's events from the tennis game to Randy's postoperative conversation with Kathy. Sitting in the bed with his right eye beneath a bandage, he had told her how worried he was about losing his sight and subsequently his career as well. He had never before opened up to her with such earnest candor. The conversation caused her a great deal of anxiety, but she appreciated his sharing his worst fears with her. It drew them decidedly closer.

Joan listened intently, concerned about Randy's sight and career, as well as her roommate. She shuddered at the possibility of sight loss and subsequently career loss for her friend. She recognized that her emotional response to the potential loss for her friend was something she would have to compartmentalize when dealing with a patient. *Not sure I can do that.*

Before they knew it, the doorbell was ringing to announce that the pizza had arrived. Joan answered the door and, having received the pizza, placed it on the coffee table.

"What would you like for a beverage, my lady?" she asked Kathy with an exaggerated flourish, trying to lighten the mood.

"Okay, okay. I am fine. I don't need to be waited on, but do we have any ginger ale?"

"In fact, we do," Joan answered from the kitchen. "Vernor's or Seagram's?"

"My goodness! We even have a choice of ginger ales. What a posh place!"

"Jay likes Vernor's."

"I see. Well, I'll take Seagram's."

"One Seagram's coming up."

The girls ate, talked, and basically calmed each other down while further building the bond between them. They had just cleared the meal's dishes when the phone in Joan's room rang. As she dashed to answer it, Kathy called out, "I'm going to bed. I'm sort of done for the day. See you in the morning."

"Hi, Joan."

"Hi. Mom, how are you?"

"Fine. Do you have a minute to talk?"

"Sure. I'm sitting in bed and happy to chat before calling it a day."

"Adam has an interview at the University of Chicago law school! We're all very excited, especially Adam and me," Liz said.

"That's great! When are you coming out?"

"Still to be determined, but soon."

"Terrific! Among other things, we have to go birding. They're coming back. Last week, I saw an eastern towhee. On our way to play tennis yesterday, Kathy and I saw a goldfinch and a blue-gray gnatcatcher, so the migration has started. Bring your binos."

"Of course. How's Jay?"

"Fine. We played mixed doubles with Kathy and Randy yesterday." Joan then told her mother about the tennis game leading to the discovery of Randy's retinal detachment and his surgery this morning.

"Oh dear! I hope he's all right."

"Yeah. We all do. Evidently the surgery went well, so that sounds good."

"How about your patient with her baby under the bili lights?"

"Anna has been discharged home."

"I bet that was a relief."

"Yes. It was, and I haven't heard anything further."

"No news may be good news in this case."

"I think so."

"I have a bit of news. I think I mentioned before that I had been seeing someone. Well, I still am," Liz said.

"Who?"

"His name is Matt. Your uncle John introduced us. He was a law school classmate of John's. They had lost track of each other and met at a reunion. He's a recent widower, one year. It's been a long time for me, so it was a little awkward between us at first. We're more comfortable now, but it still feels like foreign territory. Anyway, he'll be coming to Chicago with us. I hope you like him. I do."

"That's great, Mom. You'll meet Jay, as well, and I hope you like him too." She grinned at the concept of mother and daughter in similar circumstances. "Does Matt like birding?"

"He does. So it's terrific that we share that."

"Does he like history?"

"Sure. Most lawyers do, to one degree or another. Also, guess what?"

"What?"

"His great-great-uncle is Thomas Wentworth Higginson!"

"Wentworth? Oh my! He's a shoo-in." Joan remembered her mother's great interest in this historical figure, but she was somewhat skeptical. "How can that possibly be? What are the odds?"

"When your family scion is one of the early settlers in New England, there are a lot of people related to you, so the odds may not be so low. You're right, however. It does give him an edge," Liz said, seemingly very satisfied with herself. "I really do enjoy being with him."

Joan imagined her mom grinning ear to ear. "Well, that sounds wonderful, Mom. So glad you are happy and thrilled that you guys are coming out soon. Let me know when, as soon as you know."

"Sure. Get a good night's sleep, Joanie."

"You too. Love you, Mom."

"Love you."

Joan hung up the phone.

Hmm, I'm thrilled my mother has found someone and she's happy, but I'm not sure how I feel about this guy.

Her dad had died when she was three. She remembered a big man picking her up and tossing her in the air, and it had been great fun but not much more.

I'm not concerned about my dad being replaced. Rather, it has just been the two of us, and I'm not sure I want to share my mom. How's this going to work?

It helped that Matt was a good friend of her uncle John's.

He's not a stranger, so to speak. I do hope he can share. Of course, she has to make her own decisions, so I guess I'll just have to go with it and be happy for her. The fact that he is related to Wentworth, a key figure in Mom's area of study, is rather surreal!

Why is the morgue always located in the basement of the hospital? The basement, a part of the daunting tunnel system.

It was the first day of her pathology rotation, which met in the morgue. While walking to the hospital, she spotted a hermit thrush scrabbling around at the edge of some striking pink azalea bushes in full bloom. *Well, you have a lovely place to gather your lunch. I, on the other hand, have to spend my morning in the bowels of the earth.*

Descending the stairs from the second floor where she had left her coat in her locker, she felt the cold, damp air of the subterranean floor rise up, increasing step-by-step as she descended. She arrived at the tunnel, shivering. Looking both ways, she proceeded to the morgue. At least the door had signage designating it as MORGUE. Better than the rest of the tunnel, which was a smelly, unlabeled, confusing labyrinth. However, the bold black letters were definitively grim in their message. She had not been looking forward to this rotation, and now here it was.

She pushed open the door to find not much better lighting than in the tunnel. It was dim in addition to being dank. No one was there. How could that be? This was where they were supposed to meet on the first day of her pathology rotation. Her shivering increased. She looked about and saw two stainless steel tables in the middle of the room. One wall consisted of three rows of large metal drawers with central handles, which she knew contained bodies. She stood there with her anxiety level rising by the second, not sure of what to do next.

I'm not going to wait here by myself.

At that moment, the handle of the door leading to the tunnel moved, and her heart began to beat at an incredible rate. Before she simply collapsed on the floor, a friendly face peeked around the edge of the door.

"Oh, there you are, Joan," Peter Palmer, her pathology resident for this rotation, said. "They changed the first-day location to the pathology microscope lab on the first floor. I figured you would be here. I'll take you up."

Joan's heart slowed its rate of beating, but it was still in high gear. "Thank you. I was wondering where everybody was," Joan responded as she breathed a sigh of relief that she tried to hide.

They made their way through the tunnel and up the stairs to the lab, which had several rows of benches holding microscopes. It had windows and was actually sunny. What a mood changer!

Pete provided the tissue sample slides, which she was to study, along with the path lab manual for her to use as a reference. "Why don't you work with these for a while? Dr. Dragger's talk will begin in about an hour in the lecture hall. I'll meet you there and then take you to the morgue for your introduction. Any questions?"

"No, I think I'm fine." She smiled.

I'm fine all right! Good grief, what a morning! I was scared out of my wits. So much for an auspicious introduction to pathology. I'm alone in this room, too, but it's quite different from the morgue. There are windows with sun shining through. It's not cold and damp and smelly.

She then got down to business and turned on the light in the microscope, opened her slide box, and put the first slide under the scope. It was normal muscle tissue and appeared quite beautiful with its orderly array illuminated and magnified by the microscope.

She opened the lab manual to read about the structure of muscle tissue. Her heart rate continued to slow as she relaxed into learning mode.

The hour passed quickly. She closed her manual, replaced the slide in its box, turned off her scope, and left for the lecture hall.

The first lecture by Dr. Dragger was a historical journey of the study of pathology, and Joan found it thoroughly engaging. She had inherited an interest in history from her mother and always liked to hear about the development of any discipline. The creation of the microscope itself was pivotal to the study and understanding of the tissues and cells that made up the body. Pete had explained earlier that there were conflicting thoughts on its development. Galileo Gallilei had received credit for it in 1690, while a Dutch father and son team, Hans and Zacharias Janssen, had evidently invented the first compound microscope in the late sixteenth century.

Joan had responded, "When things occurred that long ago, sometimes the story gets confused. I'm glad the microscope was developed. I'm sure my favorite part of pathology will be studying tissues through the scope rather than visiting the morgue."

At the end of the lecture, she spotted Pete, who was looking for her to give her the morgue introduction.

"Shall we take the stairs?" he asked.

"Sure. I'm happy to get some exercise after sitting for a few hours in both the microscope lab and the lecture."

They made their way down the stairs and into the tunnel. Joan found herself looking in both directions before entering.

Pete didn't seem to notice. He was beginning his introduction to the morgue. "You can come here any time to review what you have learned. It's always open."

Oh, terrific. I'm really glad to hear that. I'll be coming here frequently to make up my work. My favorite time will be midnight, I'm sure.

Pete went on. "You will learn the basic techniques for removing and weighing and studying the organs. The chief pathologist is a master at preparation of the body, and he also has training in forensic pathology. I am very thankful to be studying under him. The bodies are kept in these drawers. They are refrigerated for tissue preservation."

He is really excited about his chosen field. I have to be careful about what I say. I am still at the "this is ghastly" stage, but I'm sure there's a lot to learn, and I'd better get over it. I appreciate that Pete is enthusiastic. That should help me leap the hurdle.

The tour completed, Pete held the door open, and the two entered the tunnel together.

Joan took the elevator to the eleventh floor to meet Jay for lunch. He was already sitting at the table by the window with lunch for two.

He reached up and took her hand as she sat down with him. "How was pathology?" he asked.

"Mixed. I like the microscopic study but am not convinced about the morgue. Pete, my resident, is very enthusiastic, so that should help with my initial low estimation of that dank and dreary place. How's Randy?"

"Feeling better this morning. The bandage is off, and he's light sensitive, but he should be able to go home. I think he's going to stay at your apartment with Kathy tonight. I was thinking that I would stay with you, and then he would have an in-house ophthalmologist."

"Is that the only reason for staying with me?" she asked coyly.

"Well, maybe not, but can't I have more than one reason?"

"I guess," she said nudging his shoulder. "Oh, I almost forgot. My family is coming to visit. My cousin is having a law school interview. My mom is joining my aunt and uncle for the trip, *and* she is bringing a boyfriend."

"Wow!"

"Yes, wow!" She then told him about Liz's latest news and that she wanted Matt to meet her family.

"Okay. I'm anxious to hear the whole story tonight at your house."

"I'm anxious to tell you the whole story tonight at my house." She grinned, squeezing his hand.

SEVENTEEN

RED-WINGED BLACKBIRD: *Agelius phoeniceus*
A blackbird with red shoulders that nests in virtually every wet, brushy, or marshy area within its wide range.

May 1980, Chicago, Illinois

JOAN ARRIVED AT HER apartment earlier than usual and went out for a run with Rusty to clear her mind and take care of his needs. She heard the buzz of its chatter song before she saw the red-winged blackbird swinging on a blade of tall grass at the edge of the marsh bordering the lagoon. He was displaying his bright red epaulet badges to defend his territory. Rusty showed no interest, so the badges reverted to their coverable state, but the bird continued his song, reveling in his own voice.

The day had been a mild one, and the temperature was still around sixty degrees. Both refreshed, she and Rusty turned a corner on their way back. In the distance, Joan saw Kathy and Randy heading toward the apartment. They were walking slowly, arm in arm.

I hope this turns out well. What a shame it would be for him if it doesn't. Let's see. Maybe we can order something tasty for dinner. I think he likes Thai food.

At the apartment building, she let Rusty off the leash, and he bounded up the stairs.

Rusty, you've got more energy left than I do.

"Hi, guys. How's the patient?"

"Okay, I guess. Looking forward to seeing better," Randy said with a grim smile.

"How about Thai food? I thought I could call for delivery. Pad Thai and drunken noodles, a couple of orders of each?"

"Sounds good," Randy said as Kathy nodded in agreement while squeezing his arm.

Jay knocked just after Joan had placed the call and fed Rusty. She went to the door and received a lasting, back-bending kiss.

"Well, so, how are you?" she asked. "We're planning on Thai. I just ordered it."

"Sounds great! How's Randy?"

"See for yourself. He's in the living room."

"Hey, man. How goes it?" Jay asked the "in-house" patient while pulling his penlight from his pocket.

"Let's wait till after dinner for any inspection by the ophthalmologist," Randy begged. "I'd rather have a full stomach."

"Sure. No problem. Does anyone want a beer?" Jay asked while walking to the kitchen.

The other three nodded yes.

"Okay. Four beers for the crowd." Walking back with the bottles, two in each hand, he said, "The Cubs did pretty well today. Beat the Giants 15 to 9."

"Sounds like a good game," Randy responded. He looked at his beer. "This hits the spot!"

"Do you have any guac, Joan?" asked Jay.

"We do. In the fridge."

"Chips?"

"Yes. I'll help you." She moved into the kitchen with him.

"How about a little kiss?" he asked while swooping her up with his left hand and holding her chin with his right hand.

She smiled back up at him, shaking her head a little.

"I take that as a yes."

Following this, they set out guacamole and corn chips in two bowls, each carrying one back to the living room.

"So tell me about the game. I just saw the first inning on the hospital TV," Randy said.

There was an inning-by-inning discussion of the game by Jay, to which Randy listened intently.

Joan and Kathy liked watching Cubs games, too, but Joan was updating Kathy on her family's visit and her mom's news.

"That's wonderful that she has found someone," Kathy said.

"Yes, it is, though, as I've told Jay, I may have some mixed feelings."

"That's not unexpected. Sounds like a normal response to me."

The doorbell rang announcing the food had arrived, and they were all glad to hear Randy respond, "Great! I'm really hungry!"

Food and beer finished and dinner plates cleared to the kitchen, Joan and Jay drifted toward her bedroom, wanting, among other things, to give Randy and Kathy some space. They bid their good nights and glided into her room.

As the door closed, he gently touched her neck and then wrapped her snugly in his arms. She wrapped right back. The luscious kiss lasted a long time. A pause, and then things accelerated. Clothing was discarded, and two bodies hit the bed simultaneously, held together in a frantic clutch. Snuggling, kissing, touching, and coming together voraciously was followed by quietly lying on their backs and melting into the bed like the relaxation that follows a long, deep sigh, only bigger, much bigger! They lay next to each other, her head on his arm, and slept a little.

After some time had passed, they woke, and Joan, who was still mulling over her first day in pathology, began to explain the details of her experience to Jay.

"Now, how is this different from anatomy lab first year?" he asked.

"Let me count the ways," she said defensively. "In anatomy lab, there is a room full of first-years and an instructor. The lighting tends to be good. Everyone is beginning a new adventure together. You have lab partners sharing each cadaver and teaching each other. Yes, you are working on a human body, but it is an intense all-in group learning experience. Today, I was by myself walking through the tunnel, to which I have an aversion, and I arrived in the damp, dimly lit morgue alone and waited in that cold, steely room with bodies in the drawers that fill one wall. It was *different*."

"Okay. I capitulate. You've made your point." He followed this with a sheepish look. "Of course, you are right. I hadn't thought of it that way."

She looked at him. "No, clearly you hadn't. But I'm happy to enlighten you to other perspectives."

He smiled. "I appreciate that."

She smiled back, and they were both soon asleep.

The next morning, after walking Rusty, they traveled to the hospital together. Hand in hand.

"Is today a morgue day?" asked Jay.

They were on the second floor, having changed their clothing in the locker room.

"Yes, but I am meeting Pete in the scope lab, which is a relief."

"I'm sure," he said while walking toward the elevator. "See you at lunch."

"See you then." *I think he's finally coming around to understand that his six-foot-three-inch, white-male view of the world is not* universal. *I do like him a great deal, but hopefully this awareness can expand further.* In part, she was trying to deal with her own fears, and in part, she recognized the true difference in their perspectives.

She found Pete setting up the teaching slide sets along with the lab manuals in the microscope laboratory.

"Hi, Joan. You can start with heart muscle and then move to other major organs in the order presented. The first slide in each group is the normal tissue with the subsequent slides being examples of abnormal pathology. Dr. Dragger's lecture will begin in an hour and a half. I'll meet you after that in the lecture hall, and we will go to the morgue together."

As he was explaining the schedule, other students shuffled into the room and were getting their microscopes ready as well.

"Okay. Sounds good," Joan said, turning on her microscope and placing the slide on the platform beneath the lens.

Joan was finding this part of her rotation fascinating. Again, the warm incandescent light shone on the organized structure of heart muscle tissue. It glowed at her through the oculars. Moving on, she viewed the cross sections of arteries and veins with their difference in wall thickness. The normal tissue was the most aesthetically pleasing with its ongoing repeats of rows of glistening muscle fibers. The disarray of the diseased tissue leaped out in contrast. The time flew by, and soon she was making her way to the cardiovascular system lecture. Spending time with her heart muscle slide made a smooth transition to this lecture and enhanced her understanding.

That finished, she found Pete, and they were off to the morgue. She was glad to be going with him and not meeting him there. As they entered the morgue, that same chilling feeling encompassed her, but at least she wasn't alone. Two other students joined them. There were quiet introductions, and then the three students placed themselves around one of the steel tables where a postmortem exam was taking place. The incision had been made, and the organs were being removed. Occasionally students' eyes met and grimaces were shared, but these were hidden from the instructors. No one wanted to appear anything but professional and objective. Joan was weak-kneed, but at least there were people around with whom to share the experience.

The procedure was cut short when the pathologist was called to the OR to prepare a frozen section for the head of surgery, who needed information on the aggressiveness of the tumor which he had resected in order to plan how wide a margin to remove. The students went with the professor to observe the preparation of a frozen section. Joan paged Jay to let him know she would not be at lunch and proceeded to the operating room.

On the way, Pete explained that the frozen section was used primarily in oncological surgery to separate a benign from a malignant tumor. The quality of the samples was not as good as the standard formalin-fixed paraffin-embedded tissue. However, it was quick and provided information while the patient was still on the operating table and decisions needed to be made. In this case, when the path report was read to the surgeon, it concluded the tumor was malignant and the surgeon needed subsequent frozen section preparation after each additional resection to determine whether there was any residual cancerous tissue. By the time the surgery was completed, it was late afternoon.

Joan was leaving the OR suite when she heard a Code Pink. It sounded like it was a patient from the nursery, so Joan beelined it to the fourth floor of the women's hospital. When she arrived at the nursery, Jackie, the head nurse, was directing personnel to search in various areas. Joan went to the mother's room and found it to be empty. She reported back to Jackie, who was shocked to see her there.

She turned to Joan. "What are you doing here? Glad to have help, but you are not assigned to the nursery. You were in the middle of the Jennings baby search. Do you get off on this sort of thing or something?"

Joan was completely taken aback. "No. I thought I might help."

"The last thing we need is extra people hanging around in an emergency."

Joan had not remembered this side of Jackie. She seemed completely out of line.

Joan thought it was probably best to make herself scarce, so she did. Having left the hospital, she walked toward her apartment. The late afternoon was sunny. That helped, but it was insufficient to completely elevate her mood.

I wonder what that was all about. I understand Jackie is tense during a Code Pink, but that seemed over the line. I don't remember her being like that when I rotated through peds. I really was just trying to support the search.

When she arrived at the door to her apartment, Rusty was barking a greeting and the phone was ringing.

"Hello."

"Hello, Joan. This is Sarah. I just wanted to let you know that Anna and I are fine and that one of my sister's friends, Shirley Bragg, is due soon and will be coming to the hospital any day now."

"Hi, Sarah. Glad to hear from you. I just heard a Code Pink. She's not there already, is she?"

"No. She's not. She hasn't had her baby yet."

"Good to know. I'm happy to have an update on you and Anna and to know that you're doing well!"

"Yes. She's eating up a storm and growing. The pediatrician says everything is going well."

"Terrific! And your sister, Jill, and her baby?"

"Doing great."

"Well, thank you for calling and keeping me in the loop. I'll watch for Shirley. Hope to talk to you soon."

As soon as Joan was off the phone, she dropped onto the couch and sighed. *I'll have to ask Erin for follow up on today's Code Pink. I don't want to make extra trips to the nursery and run into Jackie. She was really quite vile.*

Rusty barked at the door, and soon Kathy walked in.

"Hi. Want to go for a run together with Rusty?" Joan asked. "I need to defuse."

"Sure. Just let me get changed."

"I'll go put on my running gear as well. By the way, how are you? How's Randy?"

"I'm fine. Randy went to his surgeon this morning. Things are progressing well. He spent the day at his apartment reading as much as he could without causing his eye to feel worse or getting a headache. He said his vision was better than yesterday."

"All you can ask for. Be right out," Joan said as she walked to her bedroom.

Attired for running, the three of them headed for the lagoon path. "This feels great!" Joan said halfway out. "Thank goodness for the joy and cleansing of running!"

"I'm with you on that."

Joan began recounting the events of the day, especially the Code Pink and Jackie's comments.

"That seems a little bizarre," Kathy responded. "But maybe she just freaked out and lost it."

At that point, Joan spotted Erin walking her dog. "Kath, I want to catch Erin and ask about today's Code Pink."

"Hey, Erin," she called.

"Oh, hi. I didn't see you guys."

When asked, Erin responded that she had heard the all clear and evidently it was just a miscommunication. Both baby and mother were found and fine.

"And how's your sister?"

"Anxious and sad. Losing two babies and not being able to start another is taking its toll. I just don't want her to do anything desperate. I'm sure she'll be able to get pregnant again and have a baby. She's just not so sure at this point."

"Sorry to hear that. Keep listening to her."

"I will, but you don't fully understand. My sister has real problems. Not like you guys whose major issue is what specialty to choose. She's losing babies! They're dying! She's having trouble becoming a mother."

"We're so sorry."

Erin turned, "Come on Lily, we have to go."

Joan and Kathy looked at each other puzzled.

Arriving at the top of their stairs, and completely out of earshot, Joan turned to Kathy. "What was that all about? I'm not sure what she means by desperate, but I'm sure her sister is distressed."

Kathy said, "Erin's distressed." Joan nodded in agreement, but still somewhat dumbfounded.

Climbing the stairs, after running, both were sufficiently sweaty to warrant showers. Joan fed Rusty first, and then the roommates went to their respective rooms to relax in warm water.

Dinner was leftover Thai. They had purchased an exuberant amount of each dish the previous night.

That's okay. This way, we just have to reheat in the micro and, voilà, dinner!

They had just carried plates to the kitchen when Rusty started barking, and then the doorbell rang.

"Expecting anyone?" asked Joan as she walked to the door.

"Nope."

She looked through the peephole. *Oh no, the police again.* The same two very big Chicago cops stood outside the door.

"Good evening," they said with badges held out for Joan to view. "Can we come in? We just have a few questions."

"Sure," Joan responded as she walked toward the living room. "This is my roommate, Kathy."

Kathy nodded. "Would you like a cup of coffee or a Coke?"

"Coke would be great," they both said.

"What can I help you with?" asked Joan.

"We're just updating our files. We heard that you have talked with Sarah."

Joan was shocked. "That just happened this afternoon!"

The two policemen smiled knowingly back at her.

"Have you tapped our phone?"

They said nothing and then, "What was the conversation about?"

"Is that legal?" Joan demanded.

"How is Sarah?" they persisted.

Joan begrudgingly conceded. "Fine. She said she and Anna were doing well and that she just called to keep me in the loop."

"Good to know. Any news of Baby Jennings?"

"No. I haven't heard anything. You know, I'm not really news central on any of this."

"Just making sure our data is complete. Thank you for your time."

With that, they both stood up and moved toward the door. Turning before walking out, the larger one cautioned, "Again, just a reminder. Don't leave town."

EIGHTEEN

YELLOW-RUMPED WARBLER: *Dendroica coronata*
Our most visible warbler, found in open woods and brushy areas,
this species often perches upright with its yellow rump exposed
while flitting up to catch flying insects.

May 1980, Chicago, Illinois

JOAN SLOWLY AWAKENED. *Another day, another dollar spent on my medical education.*

Having the police stop by in the evening always meant a sleepless night, so she lingered and was feeling less cheery than usual. Then Rusty arrived at the edge of her bed with his big wet tongue. How could she be anything but upbeat when she had a cheek full of dog saliva?

"Okay, boy, I'm up. Are you ready for a run?"

Rusty knew this word, *run*, and his tail began wagging wildly. On their way out, the two walked through the kitchen where Kathy was eating her breakfast.

"Hi, Kath. Want to join us for a run?"

"No, thanks. I have to get to the hospital for a case. I talked with Randy this morning, and he thinks he's seeing better," she said with a definite uplift in her voice.

"Sounds great! Give him a 'hi' for me."

"Will do. Have a good run."

Soon after, Rusty plummeted down the stairs. Joan followed with his leash, and they both greeted the morning, which was bright and sunny. *Just what I need.*

Joan and Rusty made their way to the path around the lagoon, where she spotted a yellow-rumped warbler. *The warblers are arriving! It must be close to May 15.* In fact, it was May 16. *Those warblers were on the money.* Joan thought about the timing capabilities of birds. Large numbers of warblers arrived in this area each year right around May 15. How they managed this was quite remarkable but still a puzzle.

Also, she had just been reading about a pair of piping plovers, just one pair that had been nesting on one of the Chicago beaches for the last three years. They had had three chicks the previous year. Banding data showed that the female wintered in Florida and the male in Texas, but they returned to their Chicago beach for nesting this year just one day apart. Amazing! And very romantic! *How do they manage that?*

Romance brought Jay to mind. She really was quite smitten, and he seemed to be as well. There had been no further talk about a girlfriend, and Joan dismissed it as a misunderstanding as she contemplated her feelings.

Love—what was it? Clearly, the plovers were hardwired for it. Humans, who thought they were in control of their own destiny, must at least, in part, be hardwired as well. Did that make it less romantic? No, she didn't think so. She looked forward to the upcoming visit of her family and their meeting Jay. Lost in this reverie, she missed seeing the dark figure who was watching her. She and Rusty rounded the last corner of the lagoon and headed back to the apartment while the man stayed at the lagoon edge and followed them with his eyes.

Having showered and fed herself and Rusty, Joan was ready for micro path lab. She nearly ran to the hospital to get there on time. The other students were busy at their microscopes when she arrived, but she had done extra work on the previous day, so she wasn't behind, and she had really needed that run and some free-thinking time. She knuckled down to work and was soon totally immersed in liver pathology. Engrossed, she startled when Pete spoke to her.

"Joan. Oh, sorry, didn't mean to surprise you. Just wanted to let you know that we will meet after the path lecture in the morgue for the forensic pathology demonstration."

She acknowledged the message with a head nod so as not to disrupt her chain of thought.

Dr. Dragger's lecture was on pathologic changes in the liver due to the toxicity of alcohol. While listening, Joan thought of her pediatrics resident, Jim, discussing the social aspects of medicine and their importance in the cases of shaken baby syndrome. Here was another example. Alcohol was a known toxin for the liver, resulting in cirrhosis and organ failure, and yet people still drank to excess and killed themselves slowly.

You'd think we humans would be hardwired not to do that, if for nothing else but the survival of the species. Difficult to fathom without taking into consideration the social aspects and, in this case, addiction.

The lecture completed, she headed down to the morgue for the forensic pathology demonstration. She took her place at the steel table, which had the internal organs spread out on it.

The pathologist lifted each and explained its gross anatomy. "The microscopic anatomy has been investigated on each of these specimens and found to be normal. So what was the cause of death?"

He moved toward one of the drawers as he stated that they had found signs of a ligature compressing the patient's neck. This was a basically healthy person who was strangled and then was disposed of in water, so there were signs of bloating, but the cause of death was not drowning. Water was not found in the lungs because she was dead before her body was submerged.

As Joan walked toward the drawer, she felt a cold chill of recognition. In the drawer, beside the cadaver, was a piece of floral material that she had seen before. She began to shake and didn't know whether she was going to vomit or pass out. She did neither, but the body was unmistakably that of Denise.

Pete saw the pasty white of Joan's skin and her uncontrollable shaking.

He moved quickly toward her and led her out of the morgue. "Don't worry," he said, standing in the tunnel with her. "This is not an uncommon reaction to a forensic pathology demonstration. It is really pretty gross, and you gradually develop a tolerance for it. You will be fine."

"You don't understand. I *know* her. She was the mother of one of my patients," Joan stammered.

"Oh, crap. Joan, that sucks!" Pete said with a grim twist to his mouth.

She looked at him and nodded weakly. "Can we get out of this tunnel?"

"Sure," he said as he led her to the nearest stairway.

They mounted the stairs to the second floor, where she removed her purse and light jacket from her locker.

"I'm going to head for home."

"Good idea. The path demo is completed by now. You saw what you needed to learn. See you tomorrow."

"See you. Thanks."

As she walked to her apartment, Joan could not get pictures of Denise out of her head. She saw her with her brother in her hospital room, alive. Then, the body in the morgue would flash vividly into Joan's mind view, the life gone from her.

How horrific! My skin feels like there are ants crawling all over me. Poor Denise. Simply ghastly! Somebody out there murdered her in cold blood, took her life and her baby. I can't fathom it. My mind just doesn't reach around this.

When she arrived home, Rusty was barking a greeting on the other side of the door.

"Hey, Rusty." She reached down and slid to the floor, hugging him around his thick neck. "You are the best doggie in the whole wide world!"

He nuzzled back, knowing that, of course, he was.

She paged Jay. The nurse who answered said he was scrubbed in the OR and would call her back at the end of the case. She called her mother, knowing she usually lectured in the mornings and worked at her desk in the afternoons, so she might be able to talk in the middle of the day.

"Oh, Mom, do you have time to talk?"

"Of course. What's up?"

Joan blurted out the morning's happenings, seeing the remnant of Denise's dress and her body, empty of organs but bloated from lagoon waters. She cried on her end of the phone, and Liz sobbed on hers. They sat in two different states, a thousand miles apart, each holding onto their receivers for dear life.

Then Liz said, "Oh, Joanie, I am so sorry that this all happened."

"Me, too, Mom. I'm going to have to help get these guys!"

"Now, Joan, be careful. You don't want to be hurt as well. Clearly, these people are capable of terrible things."

"I know. I'll be careful."

"I mean, you really *do* have to be careful."

"I know."

"We're coming to Chicago."

"When?"

"Next weekend. I was just about to call you when the phone rang. Adam's law school interview is on Friday, so we will arrive Thursday night and leave Sunday late afternoon."

"That's great! I need to be thinking of something other than Denise's horrible fate."

"Yes, you do."

"We should do some birding on Saturday. The migrating warblers have arrived!"

"Terrific! We'll have a celebratory dinner Friday night and bird on Saturday. It's so nice the warblers are there. Great timing."

"On more than one level. For the birds and for me."

"Are you doing okay, sweetie?"

"I am," Joan said with conviction.

"As we discussed, be careful. Let the police do their job. Don't try to solve this yourself."

"I won't. Love you, Mom."

"Love you, Joanie."

Joan, still feeling physically ill and emotionally exhausted, lay back on her bed and eventually fell asleep.

About two hours later, the jangle of the phone jarred her awake when Jay returned her call. She briefly told him that Denise's body was the forensic pathology presentation.

He responded that his case was completed and he would be right over with food.

Soon after, he burst through the door, with Rusty barking his greeting and boxes of Chinese takeout cascading to the floor. "Joanie, I am so sorry about all of this," he said, engulfing her in his arms.

"Me too," she said, her voice muffled by his shoulder. "I'm okay though. I'm all cried out. Let's get this food off the floor before Rusty decides he is hungry."

Jay smiled down at her. "Always the practical person."

"I don't know about that, but I *am* hungry. Thanks for bringing dinner."

They gathered up the warm boxes, none of which had opened from the fall—only the welcoming delicious scent had escaped.

"These Chinese boxes are pretty damned good," he commented. "Beer?"

"They are. Yes. Would you bring me a glass of water too?"

"Sure."

They were settled in and eating when Kathy and Randy arrived and joined them.

"How's the eye?" asked Jay.

"Doing much better. The vision is back to twenty-twenty-five, and my stereoacuity is almost normal as well."

"Terrific! So no further thoughts about having to give up your plans for orthopedic surgery."

"Right. I'm pretty much out of the woods. Amazing, the impact of seemingly small things," Randy answered.

"As the ophthalmologist representative in our group, I will reiterate that nothing about the eyes or vision is a small thing," Jay said with a twinkle in his eye but a deadly serious tone in his voice.

Then Joan told them of her experience in the morgue.

"Oh, Joan, this just won't go away," Kathy said.

"It's not going to until we get these guys."

"We?" All three looked at her quizzically.

"Well, the police. But I want to help in any way that I can."

"Of course," said Kathy, "but you have to be careful. It's not your job, after all."

"I know. My mom said the same thing, but this is getting more and more personal."

Jay, sitting next to her on the couch, reached over and put his arm around her. "First, you have to become a great doctor—while, of course, spending quality time with me. Then, you can solve mysteries."

She looked at him resolutely. "Sometimes, there is a temporary shift in the order of things."

"Of course," he said, recognizing that backing off could often be the best way of moving forward in any relationship.

"Some good news!" Joan added, clearing the air. "My cousin has a law school interview this Friday, and my family is arriving on Thursday night."

"Great!" Jay said. "Does this mean I have a date to meet them?"

"Yes. It does," she said, looking up at him.

"I'm ready," he said, playfully squeezing her shoulder.

Kathy and Randy were starting to clear dishes and prepare for an early night. While they were in the kitchen, Jay took advantage of their privacy to give Joan a deep and enthusiastic kiss followed by an intense stare from those surprisingly blue eyes.

She was feeling so much better than earlier in the day, and this was due in no small part to Jay. This guy really was something special.

All four said their good nights and moved toward their respective bedrooms.

Mental and physical exhaustion combined to contribute to a deep, dense sleep, but as soon as Joan reached that state...

"Aunt Eleanor! Good to see you. Where are we going tonight?"

"We can stay here and chat in my car. You have helped me on previous meetings, so it is my turn to help you. Since you are on your pathology rotation and spending time in the morgue, I think we should talk about death. My good friend Emily Dickinson has a wonderful poem about it. Her first collection of poems was published in 1890 by her friend and mine, Thomas Wentworth Higginson, and contained this poem:

THE CHARIOT
Because I could not
stop for Death–
He kindly stopped for me–
The Carriage held but just Ourselves–
And Immortality.

"It goes on, but this is the essence that I wish to convey to you. You will witness death in your chosen profession more than most people do. It is viewed as the enemy by many physicians. It is what we fight against to maintain health and life for our patients. I think it helps to address it and compartmentalize it early on. It is a natural part of being human, of being any living organism, for that matter.

"We are given life. Time passes, and our bodies age and are no longer capable of sustaining our lives. This is reality. We, and our patients, deserve a full life and a dignified passage on from life as we know it. Our profession seeks this goal for those in our care. I certainly don't intend to preach but rather to share with you my long experience as a physician to help you understand this most difficult eventuality that we all must face."

NINETEEN

BALTIMORE ORIOLE: *Icterus galbula*
The male is a distinctive bird with an orange breast with black head and two wing bars. They are found in broad-leaved woods.

May 1980, Chicago, Illinois

THE NEXT MORNING, Joan and Jay both awakened to sequential visits from Rusty's soggy tongue.

Death. I understand accepting the concept and appreciate Aunt Eleanor's help with that, but what I have been thinking about lately is that life was taken from Denise. Her body didn't age and become incapable of sustaining itself. It was broken and destroyed by an evil person. I suppose as a future physician, I should pass the baton and let the police do their job, which begins at the point mine ends. Her thoughts were interrupted by . . .

"Joanie. Are you awake?" asked Jay as he touched her shoulder and kissed her on her cool neck, which was exposed above the covers.

"Yes. Good morning," she murmured. "Hope you slept well. I was just musing about my dream with Aunt Eleanor, but I guess there's no time for that now. We'd best get up and go for a quick run with Rusty."

They both donned running clothes, and off they went. The morning was a crisp sixty degrees with a slight breeze, just right for running. Rusty was ahead while they rounded the lagoon and saw Erin running with her dog, Lily. When they reached each other, they all ran in place, and the two dogs nosed each other, sniffing here and there with wagging tails.

Erin said, "We have a new baby in the nursery, Baby Boy Bragg. His mother, Shirley, is a friend of Sarah's sister, Jill."

"Oh yes," Joan said. "I remember Sarah telling me Shirley was due soon. Did everything go okay with the delivery?"

"Yes, mother and baby are fine. All's quiet in the nursery. No *uncle* has come to visit them. Just wanted to update you on that."

"Great. Thanks. See you."

Jay turned to Joan as they continued on. "Good to know."

"Yes. I'll have to stop up to see her. I told Sarah I would."

After arriving home, they each showered, dressed, and had a quick breakfast.

While at their respective lockers at the hospital, Jay said, "See you at lunch at twelve thirty?"

"Sounds good. See you." Joan smiled back at him.

With that, she was on her way to the micro path laboratory and her slides for the day. *I really do enjoy this part of pathology.*

She placed the pancreatic tissue slide on the platform of her scope. She was totally engrossed in the beautiful pink and blue pattern of the hematoxylin and eosin-stained tissue shining up at her through the oculars of her microscope when she heard:

"Code Pink is now in effect. Patient is a two-day-old infant. Patient last seen in the fourth-floor nursery of the women's hospital. If patient seen, contact security services immediately."

Oh my God! The baby ring is at it again!

She got up and ran to the door where she met Pete, who was just coming to the lab to check on the students.

"Pete, I'm going to the nursery to see if I can help."

"You're taking the tunnel?"

"It's the quickest way."

"I'll just let the other students know. Then I'll follow you."

Joan was halfway down the first flight when he finished speaking. As she entered the tunnel with its cold, musty smell, she saw a figure in blue scrubs coming toward her from the women's hospital. Running in his direction, she noted that he was carrying something. What was it?

My God! He has a baby!

She continued to run toward him, and then he took a side tunnel. When she reached the juncture, she could still see him.

He had dropped something, maybe a blanket, and had slowed down to pick it up. An avid runner, she was gaining on him.

He looked up and growled. "Get away!"

She persisted. He took another side tunnel. When she rounded the corner, he was there, looking at her with a raised left fist while holding the baby in his right arm. She looked straight at his face with its scrawny black beard, sweaty mustache, and his small, beady, evil eyes.

He smiled and showed his crooked, yellow-brown teeth as he spat out, "Scram. This is none of your business."

In the brief seconds she had, she was trying to glean any clue that would identify him. Then, she saw it. The wrist of his raised fist had a blue tattoo. It was the face of some kind of dog, with teeth bared. A hyena? She couldn't tell, but it was a menacing dog creature—that much she knew. Also, each of his four fingers on that hand had small tattoos of dog paws.

How odd.

He moved to strike her, but she dodged, and he lost his balance, just a little.

She couldn't try to knock him down. He was holding the tiny baby.

In that brief instant, she heard feet pounding the stone floor of the musty tunnel. Coming toward them? Was it Pete?

She turned to avoid the villain's reach and shouted, "Pete, call security!"

Hearing this, the man turned and ran away from her, farther down the side tunnel. Leaving some space to avoid him turning and grasping her, she pursued him. She saw him open a door, presumably to a stairwell, and enter. In the maze of the tunnel, she was not at all sure which building they were under. Where did this stairway lead? When she reached for the door handle, the door flew out and slammed against her shoulder.

He had been waiting for her behind it!

She was knocked to the ground and stunned for a moment. Trying to gather her thoughts, she again heard footsteps and shouted out, presumably to Pete. The footsteps stopped and then began again. He must have heard her and changed directions to find her.

Or maybe this was not Pete but an accomplice. She pushed that thought away. If that were the case, then why would the baby snatcher have run when she shouted out before? This time, there was no one on the other side of the door, and it opened easily. She decided to mount the stairs in pursuit. She found herself in the basement of the new pediatric hospital, next to the laundry with no one in sight. She had lost him.

Frantically, she searched for a wall phone to call security and let them know she had seen someone running in the tunnel with a baby. After Joan sent out the alert, Pete breathlessly burst through the same door. She updated him as they walked through the basement to confirm that the culprit was no longer there.

"Pete, we've notified security, but I think we should call the police."

"Won't security do that?"

"Yes, but I have been speaking to the police about this whole baby-for-sale ring."

"I'm not sure I know what you are talking about."

"Sorry. It's a long story. I'm going back to the phone to call the police and page Jay." Joan had the card with the police officer's contact number in her wallet.

She called his number on the wall phone and was told the two officers were not available. They were working on a case and would get back to her. She tried to explain that she was calling about that same case but got nowhere. Frustrated, she simply left a message. Pete stayed with her until Jay called back. Picking up the ringing phone, Joan blurted out the tunnel chase scene to Jay.

"Where are you?" he shouted back.

"In the basement of the new pediatric hospital near the laundry. I want to stay here to meet security."

"I'll be right there."

As Joan turned from the phone, she was startled to be facing Nurse Jackie.

"What are you doing here?" she growled.

"I am waiting for security," Joan stammered.

"Why are you in the middle of every Code Pink? Every single one! This can't be just a coincidence."

Joan responded by modifying the truth only slightly. "I was in the tunnel and saw a man carrying a baby after I heard the Code Pink."

"You aren't in pediatrics and yet I find you in the basement of the pediatric hospital. Aren't you in pathology now?"

Joan thought it surprising that the nurse knew what rotation she was on. "I followed him here. I started in the main hospital."

"I'm putting you in my Code Pink report. You seem to be involved in some way. There is too much here for coincidence."

The security detail arrived at the same time Jay did.

Nurse Jackie turned, gave Joan a stony look, and said, "I'm going back to the nursery. I don't want to leave Erin on her own any longer."

"What was that about? Are you all right?" Jay asked.

"I'm fine. My shoulder just got banged by the door, and I'm a little sore from being knocked to the ground."

"Knocked to the ground! What happened?"

"Yes, what happened?" the security officer asked.

Joan recounted the series of events from the announcement of the Code Pink to the present. They all listened without interrupting until she said, "I know how to identify him."

"What do you mean?" asked the officer.

"His tattoos on his left wrist and hand." She then described them in meticulous detail and made a drawing as well.

"Thank you. This is very helpful. Here's our extension in case you think of anything else. I'm sure you know the police will be contacting you as well," the security officer said.

"Yes. I expected that," she said with less dread than on previous occasions.

The members of the security detail nodded.

She turned to Jay, who gave her a hug and held her hand as they walked back through the tunnel to the main hospital.

"Are you really all right?" he asked, kissing her on the cheek.

"Yes. I'll probably have a bruise on my shoulder and maybe a few other places. I'm a little shaken but fine, and glad I got a good look at him. Nurse Jackie, however, is another story."

"What do you mean?"

"She is threatening to write me up in her review of the Code Pink. Says it is too coincidental that I appear at the scene of all the codes. I don't get it. Where is she coming from?"

"But you have gathered some really useful information."

"You're right. I don't understand her reaction, but it is unsettling in light of the police considering me a murder suspect as well."

"As we've discussed, they probably don't really think you are a suspect. The case will be helped immensely by your new information. They gave you a contact phone number. Why don't you call them this time to make it clear you are trying to cooperate with the investigation?"

"I did. I called them before I called you, but they weren't there so I left a message."

"They were probably here."

"You're right. I'm sure they will contact me."

"Do you want to have some lunch?"

"Maybe. I am a little shaken, but it will be good to sit down."

They had reached the main hospital and took the elevator to the eleventh floor and the cafeteria. Jay selected a tuna salad sandwich, but Joan was happy with a cup of tea. Her stomach wasn't ready for food. Further talking about the morning's events with Jay somehow relaxed her. She was feeling much better by the end of lunch and was recognizing how much she appreciated sharing life's ups and downs with him.

Following lunch, Jay returned to the eye clinic, and Joan, now able to think, retreated to the micro path lab where she could sit quietly and complete her slide set for the day. Pete was there and helped her with the questions on one of the pancreatic tumor slides in which the normal architecture of the tissue was completely disrupted. She updated him on the baby-for-sale ring and the rest of the morning's happenings. Also, though he was familiar with Denise's body and its forensic pathology, he did not know of her connection with the ring.

"You have to be kidding! Now I understand why you reacted so dramatically to the forensic demonstration," he responded when he had heard the whole tale.

"But I assure you, I am not kidding or exaggerating," she said resolutely. "The whole thing is horrific, and on some level, I am being accused of being a suspect both by Nurse Jackie and the police."

"That's probably not really the case."

"Anyway, I think the more people who know about this crime occurring in the hospital, the more likely it will be stopped."

"That sounds right. I'll keep an eye out," Pete said.

Having completed her slide set, Joan made her way home early from the hospital. She was thoroughly exhausted. It was sunny and seventy degrees outside. A Baltimore oriole flew by. *Perfect weather. The orioles have arrived for the spring and nesting. We really will have to go birding when my mom arrives tomorrow.*

She climbed the stairs to their apartment to the tune of Rusty's greeting and received an enthusiastic hello upon opening the door. "Okay, big guy, I'll take you for a brief walk."

They met Erin and Lily on their way out of the apartment. Knowing that she had been in the nursery at the time of the Code Pink, Joan told her of her experience and asked Erin about hers.

"It was Baby Boy Bragg, Shirley's baby, that was missing," Erin said.

"Oh no! There was so much happening that it never occurred to me that it might be Shirley's baby. How awful! She must be devastated."

"She was beside herself," Erin said. "Of course, to a certain extent, we all were. What *is* going on? We've lost two babies within a month! This ring has to be stopped. Thankfully, it sounds like your brave effort yielded some solid information for the police."

"I tried to call it in. I will try again from home. I'll also call Sarah. At least I have her phone number. I never even had a chance to meet Shirley." The dogs having done their duty, the two girls walked back to their apartments.

As the girls were ascending the stairs, Joan remembered Nurse Jackie.

"Erin, I almost forgot. Nurse Jackie seemed out of sorts. She said she was going to write me up as part of her Code Pink report. She seems to think I have something to do with these babies being taken. Did she say anything to you?"

"No, but she has been overly tense lately. Not surprising. I think it's because of these child abductions. She's in charge of the nursery and, of course, responsible for the babies. I think she's worried about her job and may be looking for someone to blame. She does seem to be bringing you up in conversations about the stolen babies."

TWENTY

AMERICAN ROBIN: *Turdus migratorius*
A large, conspicuous bird with a red breast, commonly seen on grassy lawns.

June 1980, Chicago, Illinois

THAT EVENING, AFTER having napped from the moment she returned to the apartment, Joan felt considerably better. She and Kathy had just sat down in the living room to eat their hamburgers, which Kathy had prepared with some tasty spices and grilled to perfection on the balcony. Finally, she had had a brief moment when she could use her cooking skills. Interrupting their first bite was a firm, insistent knock on the door.

"My guess is that's the police," Joan said through her first chew. "Their timing is impeccable, but I do want to talk to them."

"I'm going to eat this burger while it is hot, police or not," Kathy declared. "I'll grill the rest when Jay and Randy arrive."

"Sounds good," Joan said on her way to the door, dodging the barking Rusty.

Through the peephole, she saw the two very tall policemen.

"Hello," she greeted them as they went through their usual shtick of showing their badges. "Come in. Would you like a Coke?"

They both nodded.

"Kathy and I are going to eat our dinner while we talk."

"Sure. No problem," came the joint response as they sat down with the girls. "So we have heard that there was another baby abducted, Baby Boy Bragg, and that, again, you were at the scene."

"Yes, I was," Joan responded as she began the tale of her morning in the tunnel. At the conclusion, she said, "I got a good look at the man carrying the baby." She began with his facial features and then described the tattoos she had seen on his left wrist and fingers. She grabbed a piece of paper and made a drawing of the tattoos for them just as she had done for the security guards.

They responded that this was very helpful but went on to ask about why she was on the scene.

"I heard the Code Pink, and I want to help you get these guys. I was close to the tunnel and knew it would be a likely escape route."

"Nurse Jackie has spoken to us. She reported you in her Code Pink write up. She thinks you are involved in some way."

"That's ridiculous! I don't know what the story is with Nurse Jackie. For me, it's just that my patient was abducted and her mother murdered, so I want the crime to be solved. Now we have another baby who has been taken. This has to stop!"

"We agree with you on that, and the information you've provided should be very helpful."

"Also, what is puzzling to me is that these babies are linked."

"How so?"

"Some of the mothers knew each other. Shirley knew Sarah's sister, Jill, who was contacted by the baby snatchers. Shirley's baby has just been abducted. I'm not sure about Denise, but these are a group of single mothers, economically challenged without sufficient resources, vulnerable. Why and how are they targeted? The why may simply be that they are vulnerable, but the how?"

"You're right. They are linked. Also, it would be helpful to follow the chase path in the tunnel. Would you be available tomorrow to walk us through?"

"Sure. I'll be in the micro lab in the morning. If you stop by there, I'll show you where things occurred in the tunnel system."

"Okay, as always, thank you, but stay in the city until we get this crime solved."

This statement, which, of course, she had heard before, always left an uncomfortable feeling in the pit of Joan's stomach. *Good grief! I'll be very glad when this is over.*

As the two detectives left, Rusty barked his greeting to Jay and Randy, who were coming up the stairs.

"The police live at your place!" Randy declared.

"It smells great here! Where are the burgers?" Jay exclaimed.

"How many do you each want?"

"Two each," Jay responded as Randy nodded in assent.

"I am going to cook yours up now. I waited so they would be hot," Kathy promised. "And Joanie and I are going to split a second one, right?"

"Sure thing!" Joan said.

"I brought the cold beer," Jay said as he passed one to each and refrigerated the rest. "So how did it go with the police?" he asked Joan.

"Okay. I told them about the tattoos, and they seemed interested, but of course, I have to stay in town, which is just plain unsettling."

"I know, but your information may very well be the clincher to get this case solved, and that would be terrific." Since Randy and Kathy were on the balcony grilling the burgers, Jay leaned over and, hugging Joan, placed a long and sensuous kiss on her lips. "You are going to make a big difference in this case. I know it. You probably already have."

"Well..."

"I am entitled to my opinion."

"Of course."

The two balcony inhabitants arrived with the burgers.

"Great!" Jay said. "Let's eat!"

They all sat down and did just that while sharing the rest of the day's events.

Jay was on call and got called in for an emergency just as the dishes were finished. Kathy and Randy retired for the night, as did Joan just after she and Jay shared a lean-over-backward kiss at the door.

I really do like this guy. Joan felt warm all over for the first time in an emotionally and physically challenging day.

Pjs on and snuggled in bed, Joan dialed her mother's number.

"Hi, Mom."

"Hi, Joanie. We're coming in tomorrow!"

"I know. I'm so excited. And . . . I think I have made a major contribution to solving this baby-theft crime."

"How?"

Joan recounted the events of the morning, including her being slammed by the door. At which point, she noticed how sore her shoulder was. *Jeez, I guess I really did get whacked by that door.*

"So much has happened that I can't believe it was today that I chased that guy in the tunnel, but I am exhausted."

"My goodness Joan! Is your shoulder all right?"

"I was just noticing that it is tender, but I really am fine," she reassured her mother. "I'm going to call Sarah in the morning to see how she is doing and talk to her about Shirley and her baby. I still don't understand why, or especially how, these ladies are being targeted."

"Just be careful. I understand your concern and wanting to help solve these crimes, but it is not your primary job, and I don't want to see you hurt. These are vicious people."

"I know, but a phone call isn't particularly risky."

"And how are your studies?"

"I like the micro path lab, but the autopsies, especially the forensic ones, I could do without. The micro enables me to better understand the disease processes by looking at the tissues themselves, and I really enjoy the quiet contemplation and the beautiful view while peering through the microscope. I don't think I will become a pathologist, but that's okay—this study is essential to fully understanding any specialty."

"I'm sure pathology is pivotal to any aspect of medicine. How is Jay?"

"Great! I like him more and more. He becomes a bigger part of my life on a daily basis."

"That sounds good. I am enjoying becoming closer to Matt as well. I'm really looking forward to the four of us meeting."

"Me too. See you tomorrow."

Joan put down the receiver, turned out the light at her bedside, and was asleep within minutes despite her nap. It had been a very eventful day!

The next morning on her way to the hospital, she saw a robin fly by with a twig in his beak.

This guy has been with us all year, but the season has changed, and it's nest building time.

Spring, and its associated new beginnings, was always uplifting. Her reverie was interrupted by seeing Erin, who was coming in the opposite direction.

"Night shift," Erin said seeing Joan's quizzical look.

"Ah, you need to get some sleep. Have you heard anything more about Baby Boy Bragg?"

"No. Social work was brought in to help with Shirley, a totally distraught mother. The police have been by at least twice, further questioning everyone. No word on the baby."

"As I said last night, I am going to call Sarah. I'm sure she knows about this latest abduction, but if not, she should. I hope they find the baby. Oh, and how's your sister?'"

Erin shrugged. "Gotta run."

Joan was off to her locker and then the micro path lab. She had just placed the normal stomach lining slide in her microscope and was in deep concentration when the two policemen arrived. Every student in the room except Joan looked up from their microscopes and followed the two as they walked to her spot on the lab bench. She was in deep concentration so was somewhat startled by their arrival. She greeted them, and the three left the lab for the tunnel.

This is going to generate a lot of speculation among my fellow students.

She led them along the path she had followed yesterday while meeting up with and chasing the man with the baby. She carefully pointed out where he had dropped the blanket and the door with which he had hit her. When they reached the laundry in the basement of the pediatrics hospital, she showed them the phone from which she had called security and them, and then the portion of the tunnel she and Pete had searched.

At this point, she asked, "Have you learned anything more?"

"We are scouring our files for the tattoo you described. It's an unusual one, so I think we will find something, but not yet. Your guidance this morning may lead to a possible exit taken by this guy. So thank you."

"You're welcome. I'll be glad to have this case solved."

"We're with you."

No one had noticed the dark figure that trailed them through the tunnel tour and faded into a dimly lit tributary, still watching them from the depths. He started to follow Joan as she made her way back to the pathology lab but seemed to think better of it and disappeared into the darkness.

At the lab, she was greeted with many questions from her classmates. She updated them all on the series of events, thinking the best way to stop this ring was to have as many people informed as possible. Of course, an exception to this rationale would be to avoid informing someone who participated in the crime. She felt it highly unlikely that any of the medical students would be involved.

Her time in the lab was extended both by this conversation and her tour in the tunnel with the police. When she finally finished her slide set for the day, it was midafternoon. She wanted to make the call to Sarah in privacy, so she shortened her day at the hospital and walked directly to her apartment. Upon arrival, Rusty was very eager, but she told him he would have to wait until she had completed the call.

Sarah answered. "Hello."

"Hi, Sarah. This is Joan, your medical student."

"I know your voice. Hi."

"I'm just calling to check in with you. How are you and Anna?"

"We're fine. Anna is growing and doing all the right baby things, according to the pediatrician. But have you heard about Jill's friend Shirley and her baby boy?"

"Yes, I know. It's just awful." She then told Sarah about the chase in the tunnel and her description of the man and his tattoo. "Have you ever seen a tattoo like that?"

"No, but I'll ask Jill and Shirley too. I'm going to visit Shirley this afternoon. They just *have* to find her baby. She is beside herself, as you can imagine. Oh, and if you see her, please thank Nurse Jackie. She has been very good about calling Jill and me and keeping in touch about Anna and Sasha. We both appreciate her calls."

"Sure. Happy to. Be sure to touch base with me if you find anyone who has seen the tattoo."

"Will do. Thank you for checking up on us."

"You're welcome. Take care and don't hesitate to call."

Rusty was licking her knee insistently.

"Okay. We'll go for a run." Joan's running clothes on, they both bolted down the stairs and headed for the lagoon path.

The robin seen that morning was still carrying sticks for its nest.

Life goes on, thought Joan, totally engaged in her run.

She paged Jay when she and Rusty returned to the apartment. "My mom called. She and Matt are coming in on an earlier flight. Would you like to join them for pizza at Lou Malnati's restaurant tonight around six? I think it would be nice for just the four of us to get together."

"Sounds good to me. I should be finished up in clinic soon. I'll come over to the apartment and pick you up."

"Okay. See you."

Jay arrived at five thirty so they would have enough time to drive to Lou's. Joan wore a light blue and pink flowered dress with an open neck and a blue sweater.

"My, my," he said as she stepped into the car. "I can't think of when I last saw you in a dress. I like this one."

"Thank you," she said, smiling and giving him a peck on the cheek. She was surprised he noticed but glad that he did.

"We're going to Lou's on—"

"Wells Street."

"Oh yeah. Okay. I'm going to take Lake Shore Drive."

"Good. That's such a beautiful route. Thank goodness for Daniel Burnham and his colleagues who made sure the lakefront was protected for all to enjoy by setting aside that land for parks over a hundred years ago."

They drove past the Field Museum and the Adler Planetarium, and Joan drank in the beautiful view across the lake to the lighthouse and adjacent Navy Pier.

They succeeded in finding parking near the restaurant and entered to see Liz and Matt already at a table. Introductions, hugs, and handshaking were shared all around, and then Joan and Jay sat down to join them. One large thin crust with mushrooms and pepperoni and one large deep-dish spinach pizza and four beers were ordered.

Matt and Jay, encouraged and occasionally interrupted by Liz and Joan, provided brief backgrounds to the group as a way of further introduction. There was a good deal of laughter shared as anecdotes were sprinkled throughout the presentations. The conversation then moved to the present, and Joan updated everyone on the baby-for-sale ring and its horrors.

"There is a piece missing in this puzzle," Joan said. "I still don't understand *how* this ring has zeroed in on this group of women and keeps finding new mothers and attacking them."

TWENTY-ONE

BLUE-GRAY GNATCATCHER: *Polioptila caerulea*
Our most widespread gnatcatcher is a blue-gray color with white outer tail feathers. They are often found in trees and high bushes.

June 1980, Chicago, Illinois
1853, New York City, New York

JOAN AWOKE WITH a start. She was alone in her bed and heard water running.

Jay must be in the shower. That's right. He has an early case this morning. Time to get up and start the day and try to find the missing puzzle piece. I want this nightmare over with!

Composing herself, and hearing the water turn off, she headed for the bathroom. Having completed their morning ablutions, Joan and Jay joined Kathy in the kitchen.

"I have a late morning start in the OR, so I've made oatmeal!" she said with a lilting swing of the wooden spoon she held in her right hand.

"Great!" was the simultaneous response from both.

"I'll get the blueberries," Joan said.

"I want brown sugar as well. Anyone else?" Jay asked.

The girls both nodded.

"Okay. Blueberries and brown sugar for the whole house," Jay concluded.

The three sat and thoroughly enjoyed the special breakfast treat of eating together.

Jay and Joan left with Rusty in tow. Jay was headed to the OR, and Joan and Rusty for his much-appreciated walk.

Joan looked out at another spectacular day, seventy-five degrees and sunny with only a gentle breeze. *Tonight is the celebratory dinner with my whole family. I want to get things settled in my mind before that.* A blue-gray gnatcatcher landed in an adjacent tree. *That's my second one this year. They are such beautiful birds. Catch those gnats, you guys!*

Returning home with Rusty, Joan was just about to go back out again and walk to the hospital when there was a knock on the door. She looked through the peephole, and there were the two policemen.

Good grief. What now?

The usual introduction from the two cops played out.

"I have to go to the hospital," Joan said, "so we need to make this quick."

"We just have one question. Where were you the night before you found the body in the lagoon? Time of death is estimated to be the previous night."

Joan felt a pain in the pit of her stomach as she looked at them in disbelief. "You have to be kidding me. Do you really think I killed Denise! What would my motive be?"

"We're just crossing all the t's."

"Doubtless I was here in my apartment. I haven't been out in the evening in a year except to run with Rusty. Oh, and there was last night when I had pizza with my mother." She was trying to maintain her composure. "Remember, I'm a medical student."

"Can anyone confirm where you were?"

"My roommate, Kathy. Kath, are you still here?"

There was no answer. Kathy had left for the hospital while Joan was walking Rusty.

"You'll have to ask her later." She sat down in the chair by the door to make the shaking of her knees less obvious.

"Okay. Thank you for your time."

"Wait! Have you learned anything more about the baby snatcher with the tattoo?"

"No. Still working on it. You don't know him? And you are sure about the tattoo? It sounds pretty unusual."

"No! Of course, I don't know him, and I am sure about the tattoo. Good grief! You guys are unbelievable!"

"Just dotting the i's. We're going to talk to Nurse Jackie. We'll be back."

She sat in the chair for another fifteen minutes, gathering herself, and then walked to the kitchen and made a cup of tea. She snuggled with Rusty on the couch and held her mug with both hands to warm them. She felt cold all over.

She considered climbing into bed but thought better of it. The plan for the day had been that Liz and Matt, along with her uncle John and aunt Anne, were going to see a special Monet exhibit at the Art Institute while Joan completed her slide set in the micro path lab. Adam's law interview was scheduled for the morning as well. They were all going to meet at the Art Institute for lunch. Joan decided she was not going to let this morning's rendezvous with the police spoil that. She pulled herself together, gave Rusty a hug, and headed for the hospital.

In the micro path lab, she took a few deep breaths as she looked through her oculars at the villi of the small intestine. The orderly array of the tissue pleased her, and her quiet concentration in the lab helped further establish her equilibrium. She thought about paging Jay but decided against it. She just wanted to put all the crime-related chaos aside for a little bit, enjoy her studies, have lunch, and then come back and face it. She finished the slide set in record time and grabbed a cab at the front entrance of the hospital.

When she arrived in the courtyard restaurant of the museum, her family had already acquired a table and were laughing and chatting. The sun was out, and there was a soft breeze as they sat under their table umbrella, surrounded by bright red geraniums in cobalt blue pots. The waitress came by, and everyone ordered. Joan had an arugula salad with balsamic vinegar dressing, feta cheese, candied walnuts, and dried cranberries and topped with chicken, and an iced tea. She melted into her chair and enjoyed the warmth and security of her family and a delicious salad.

There was avid discussion of the Monet exhibit, especially the water lilies, and Adam reported that he thought his interview had gone well. Cheers were shared all around on that high note. Then, the questions began about Jay. How did they meet? Where was he from? How about his family? Joan fielded a few of these then assured them he would be at dinner and they could ask him directly.

Lunch finished, Joan's family went back to their hotel for a quiet afternoon before their next meal together, and she took a cab back to her apartment. Once there, she sighed deeply, shuffled into her pajamas, and slid into bed. It had been a trying interview with the police that morning. She had successfully gathered herself for pathology lab and lunch. Quite a coup! Now, however, she needed to rest and regroup before proceeding.

Laying back on her pillow with Rusty at the foot of her bed, she was quickly asleep.

"Aunt Eleanor! How are you? What's up?"

"I am taking you to New York, where in 1853, with the financial help of others, especially my Quaker friends, I set up my own independent dispensary where I could practice and where women physicians could be available for the poor. This gradually became the New York Infirmary for Women and Children, and then it expanded to the Women's Medical College of the New York Infirmary, where women could both obtain the title of Doctor of Medicine and practice and learn further from their colleagues. You see, up to that time, all women were excluded from medical companionship. Thus, we missed this means of increasing our medical knowledge. We were limited to working at small private practices, and we were not welcome at meetings. It was isolating, to say the least, but also education depriving.

"It was a hard road getting the dispensary going. There wasn't much money. We had to work elsewhere, as well as the infirmary, to cover our personal expenses, because we weren't paid for work there. However, we felt it a success, and it was. Our annual report in 1857 announced that nearly one thousand women and children had received care at our infirmary. Here we are on Bleecker Street. You can see the building on the corner of Crosby."

"Over a hundred years later, obtaining a medical degree and practicing medicine is quite different for you. I wanted you to understand how far we have come and that anything is possible if you put your mind and energies to it. Also, I know you have additionally been trying to solve a mystery recently—and succeeding, it appears. It's all well and good to keep your ethics where they should be and help in such a situation, but don't forget to keep your eye on the prize and place your medical education up front."

With that, she turned the car and headed from New York toward Chicago, where they arrived in seconds.

"Good evening, Joan."
"Good night, Aunt Eleanor. Thank you."

Joan awakened to Rusty's nose poking her right cheek. "Okay, boy. I'll take you for a walk as soon as I get dressed." While pulling up her sweatpants, Joan remembered she wanted to touch base with Jay about tonight's dinner, so she paged him. He called back in short order.

"Hi, Joanie, how are you doing?"

"Long story, but I just wanted to remind you dinner is at seven so we should probably leave around six thirty."

"Okay. Long story?"

"The police came by again with all sorts of accusations."

"That reminds me. My cousin Dick called. Apparently, they've found some suspect's fingerprints that were obtained from Denise's apartment."

"Suspect?"

"That's all I've got. He was called off to some emergency and said he would get back to me."

"Well, that's helpful. They won't be my prints. I was never there."

"Did you pick up or touch any of her stuff when you visited her in the hospital?"

"Good grief! This goes on. No, nothing except the baby. Did he have anything to say about her baby?"

"No. I'm sure someone wanted that baby enough to pay a pretty penny for her. So hopefully, she is in a happy home somewhere."

"Yes, hopefully. Okay. See you in a little bit."

"I'll pick you up at six thirty."

Rusty was nudging her leg. "Here we go, boy," she responded as she put on his leash. "Just a short one. I have to get dressed for dinner."

Down the stairs they went and off to the edge of the lagoon, at which point, Joan heard a shout.

"Joan, I have good news!" She turned to see Erin coming from the direction of the hospital. "They found Shirley's baby!"

"Wonderful! How'd you learn this?"

"The baby was brought to the peds clinic by the police to be checked for any problems from his abduction. Shirley met him there and, of course, was ecstatic. He's fine."

"Fantastic! Where did they find him?"

"That's all I know. I happened to be going by to pick up some supplies, and I saw Shirley. Happy ending!"

"At least for that part, but hey, I'll take it. Terrific! Thanks for letting me know." Joan breathed a huge internal sigh of relief.

"Of course. See you."

She and Rusty—okay, mostly Rusty—bolted up the stairs to their apartment. Joan had removed his leash and was moving toward the bathroom and her shower when she heard a knock on the door.

"Just a minute." She looked through the peephole. There were the usual suspects. She opened the door. "What's up now?"

Putting their badges away, they stated they just needed a minute.

"Well, that's all I have got. Come in."

All three sat down in the living room.

"We found the tattoo in our database and identified at least one person who has such a tattoo on his left wrist and hand. It turns out it was the right person. We had an address, and when he was arrested, the Bragg baby was found in his apartment. The baby's been examined here at the hospital and is fine and has been reunited with his mother. So thanks for the information you provided."

"Terrific! You're welcome." Joan felt the tense muscles in her scalp beginning to relax.

"He was printed, and we're looking for a match among the prints found at Denise's apartment. That murder crime is still open, as is the abduction of her baby. We'll get back to you on that and let you get on with your evening."

Getting there. She expeditiously made her way to the shower.

Jay was going to be at the door soon. Showered, she thought about what to wear. He had noticed her dress the previous night and liked it, so she picked out a yellow sundress and a slightly lighter yellow sweater in case it got cooler later in the evening. *I want and need upbeat, and yellow is upbeat.* She smiled to herself.

Jay arrived at the door just one second after she felt ready.

"Wow! You look great!" he said as she opened the door. He turned her around. "From every angle." He hugged her and said, "Are you feeling better? You look like you are."

"Your information about the fingerprints helped my mood, and I talked to Erin, who knew they had found Shirley's baby—he is fine and with Shirley now. Then the police stopped by to say they had identified the snatcher by the information I gave them about his tattoos."

"Unbelievable! A lot of good news. So things are better?"

"Yes, yes! Still a few loose ends, but much better. Let's go to dinner."

Having fed Rusty, the two of them descended the stairs to Jay's car. Traffic was a little heavy, as expected on a Friday night, but they valeted the car and entered the steak house just after the rest of Joan's family. Hugs were shared all around, and then the hostess escorted the group to their table.

Having made decisions on the menu and then ordered, Liz turned to Joan and said, "You look lovely and less stressed than I have seen you since we got here. What's new?"

"What isn't?" Joan said, and she recounted the happenings of the day.

"So things are looking up," Liz said.

Joan nodded in assent.

"Speaking of up," Adam said, "my interview went not just well but really well. Somehow, we got into a discussion about Thomas Wentworth Higginson—about whom, thanks to Aunt Liz, I knew a great deal."

"There's a great deal to know," Liz said.

"That there is," Matt piped up. "Did you know that he was my great-great-uncle?"

"I didn't know that." Adam turned to his aunt. "Should I have known that, Aunt Liz?"

"I just found out myself, but it is one of the many things Matt and I share, an admiration for his uncle."

Jay leaned over to Joan. "I don't know anything about this guy."

Adam, overhearing, said, "He was a pastor in Massachusetts whose gospel was too liberal even for Unitarians in the eighteen hundreds. His views on temperance, women's rights, labor, and slavery resulted in him losing his congregation. His house in Medford, Massachusetts, was part of the Underground Railroad."

"Wow! Sounds like he was way ahead of his time, and brave as well."

"And much more," said Liz. "His life was so rich and full that I was able to write my graduate thesis on it."

"Adam and I have heard many discussions between my mom and Uncle John about all aspects of Wentworth's life but especially his part in the Secret Six, who funded John Brown the abolitionist," Joan said.

"I'd love to hear more," Jay said.

At this point, there was a disturbance at the neighboring table. Joan looked over, and there was a heavy, red-faced man waving his arms, clearly in distress.

His wife was pulling on his arm, shouting, "Walter, Walter. What's wrong?"

"Jay, he's choking!" Joan exclaimed. No one was moving. "He needs the Heimlich maneuver!"

They both abruptly stood up and rushed to the next table. Each grabbed an arm and pulled Walter up from his chair. Jay stood behind him and wrapped his arms around, clasped his hands together, and jerked just below his diaphragm.

Liz was next to his wife explaining that they were both doctors and Jay was trying to help him. After a couple of jerks, the scallop popped out of his mouth, and he gasped for air. Jay eased him into his chair. Walter sagged there to rest. His wife was up and kissing his cheek. The rest of the family dinner party stood at their table with mouths hanging open.

Back at their own table, Matt pulled out Liz's chair for her. They all sat down and resumed eating their dinners. Joan explained the series of events that had occurred at the adjacent table.

Matt turned to Liz. "Is life with your daughter always this exciting?" he asked.

"Yes!" Jay responded, seizing the opportunity. "Always exciting!"

TWENTY-TWO

WOOD DUCK OR CAROLINA DUCK: *Aix sponsa*
A medium-sized, short legged, and long-tailed perching duck. The drake, who has a white bridle, is one of the most colorful North American waterfowl.

June 1980, Chicago, Illinois

JOAN WAS LIFTING her binoculars over her head. "Do you have a pair?" she asked Jay.

"No. Not yet, but I'll get some."

She walked into their kitchen. "Hi, Kath. Jay needs to borrow my old binos that I lent you. We're going birding with my family today."

"No problem. I put them in my top drawer." Returning with the glasses in hand, Kathy said, "You guys should have a great time. It's supposed to be sunny and seventy today."

Their plan was to meet Joan's family just behind the Museum of Science and Industry, which was housed in a building that was originally the Palace of Fine Arts in the World's Columbian Exposition in 1893. It was one of the few buildings of the White City that were not disassembled after Chicago's famous fair. A spectacular Beaux Arts gem, it had a copper dome supported by ionic columns and caryatids. There was a pond behind that often attracted water birds. This was to be the meeting place and the beginning of their hike. Joan and Jay were walking over from Joan's apartment, and the rest of the family would arrive by cab.

While waiting, Joan pointed out a pair of wood ducks to Jay. "Water birds are a good place to begin birding. They swim around, and you can get your binos on them and examine them carefully, unlike warblers, for instance, who are flitting from branch to branch, moving constantly and often obscured by leaves."

They were viewing a lovely pair of wood ducks with the male displaying his dramatically colorful breeding plumage. The female, less spectacular by far, swam just behind him, showing the characteristic white around her red eye.

"Wow," Jay said, "the male is so outrageously and elaborately decorated that he looks like his display must have been painted on his feathers."

"They are strikingly colorful and fun to watch. Here comes my family," Joan said as the group rounded the west corner of the massive museum.

Greetings were shared around by all, and then they lifted their binoculars to their eyes to get a good look at the wood ducks. There were others enjoying the pond, as well, a pair of mallards and some Canada geese. At the water's edge, Liz spotted a great blue heron—an incredible, prehistoric-looking but beautiful big blue bird—fishing at the water's edge. He was statue-like as he stood in the water up to his knees, watching for fish. Then, the viewers were mesmerized by the jerking forward of his head like an arrow leaving its bow, followed by his bill lifting from the surface with a fish. After this dramatic display, members of the group started wandering apart as each individual peered into their binos at different birds.

As they moved in amoebic fashion, one here and one there south from the pond, Liz pointed out an indigo bunting to Jay, who, once he got his binos on it, commented on the incredible iridescent blue color of this bird.

"So tell me about yourself," she said, smiling. "Just doing some due diligence for my only daughter."

"My parents, Patrick and Megan, live in Winnetka, just north of the city. My dad is a banker and so is my younger brother, Alex. My mom is a pediatrician in private practice in Evanston, close to home, and my younger sister, Lisa, is in law school at the University of Michigan."

"So everyone's in the Midwest," said Liz.

"Yes, we're a pretty close family. We try to get together every couple of weeks for dinner."

"And you've got the bases covered from medicine to law with banking in between."

Jay nodded as Matt walked up to join them.

Joan was about fifty feet away, locking her glasses onto a common yellowthroat with its black mask and intensely yellow breast, when she noted another birder about twenty feet away. She was not sure why, but she swung her binos over to get a closer look at him. She was shocked to see that his left wrist, which was exposed beyond the cuff of his jacket sleeve as he held his binoculars, had a blue tattoo of the face of a growling dog! She saw the magnified view of the fingers of his left hand as well. There were the familiar dog footprints, one on each digit, just as she had drawn them for the police after her encounter with the man running carrying the baby in the tunnel.

She shuddered and thought, *How can this be? He's supposed to be in police custody.*

She eased over to the birder to get a better look. When she was about six feet away, she asked him what bird he had found. He lowered his binoculars, looked at her face, and lunged toward her. She dodged and screamed for Jay. Startled, he looked up from his conversation with Liz and started running toward Joan. Matt and Liz queued up behind him, running toward Joan as well. The birder, noting a group in pursuit, turned and ran. Joan, recovering, began to follow him, which prompted Jay to shout, "No, Joan! Don't chase him! Wait for me!"

The "birder," having left his bicycle leaning against a nearby tree, quickly mounted it and rode off, leaving the pursuing throng standing in place and gasping for breath.

Adam, Anne, and John, who had their backs to the others, having turned toward the pond to watch the great blue heron take flight, missed the whole encounter.

Joan turned to Jay. "There's another man with the same tattoo!"

"Wait! Let's get our thoughts together. First, don't chase strange men in the park!"

"I unequivocally agree!" Liz, who had just reached the two of them, said.

Joan looked defiantly at Jay and then Liz. "You don't understand. He had the same tattoo! The tunnel guy is in police custody. This guy had the same tattoo. There's more than one perpetrator in this ring of baby thieves!"

It took a moment for this to sink in, but when it had, Jay took her arm and said, "There's a pay phone in the lobby of the museum. Let's go and call the police. Do you have the number that the two officers gave you?"

Joan fished it out of her purse and held it up for Jay to see. "Yes."

Joan and Jay moved toward the museum while Liz and Matt proceeded toward the others to update them and bring them to the museum. When next they gathered, the police had been alerted and were on their way.

Liz put her arm around Joan's shoulders. "Please promise me you won't chase these criminals. It's too dangerous."

Jay watched from Joan's other side, thankful to have Liz supporting his position.

Liz turned to the others. "This isn't the first time Joan has literally run after one of these thieves."

"Also," Uncle John said, "it appears that this one was following you, Joan. I doubt that he's a birder. He must have tracked you two from your apartment."

"I think you're right," Jay said. "They clearly know Joan has been involved with the police investigation."

"I thought my concerns about them coming after me had ended when the police arrested the baby snatcher. This was a different guy. He was considerably taller and perhaps less scruffy, though I got a better look at his left hand through the binos than his face. I was concentrating on his tattoos, which I was so shocked to see on a different person."

"Joan, Joan, Joanie, as your mother, I'm going to feel uncomfortable leaving Chicago with these people targeting you! I will not sleep a wink. I think you should take a break and come home."

"Now, Mom. I don't live alone. Kathy will be there."

"I'll be there too," Jay said with the color rising in his face. "Also, I will call my cousin, and we will request a police detail to watch the apartment."

"Jay's cousin is a Chicago-based homicide detective," Joan filled in for the others.

"I could sleep on your couch and visit some wonderful museums for a couple of weeks," Liz said.

"Oh, good grief. Let's talk to the police and make a plan after that," Joan said dreading having her mother sleeping on the couch in her apartment.

A squad car pulled up to the museum entrance, and two familiar policemen hopped out, displaying their badges.

"What's happened now?" the taller one directed his question at Joan. "No, wait. First, who do we have here?"

Joan introduced her family one by one, noting that her uncle John was a prosecuting attorney and her cousin was a law school candidate, hoping this would add some gravitas to her position. She went on to describe the incident with the other "birder," including his tattoos. The others corroborated her story as witnesses.

"Are you sure about the tattoos?" the shorter cop asked.

"Of course I am sure," Joan responded. "I looked at them with my binoculars, and as you know, I had made drawings of them before from the man in the tunnel... twice!"

The police had a few more questions about the direction the tattooed man had gone on his bicycle. After the two had signed off and left walking in that direction, Joan's family discussed what to do next.

Joan said, "If everyone is okay, let's go back and do some more birding. It's a lovely day, and I don't want to let that jerk upset our plans."

"If we do that, and I am fine with it, I am sticking right by you. None of this wandering off," Jay said while Liz nodded her head in assent.

The rest of the group agreed, and they proceeded south toward Wooded Isle and had cool-down time wandering through the gardens.

They returned to the museum a few hours later and had lunch. The afternoon was spent walking through the various exhibits, including the WWII German submarine and the replica of a human heart, both of which they could literally walk through. The two physicians in the group confirmed that the latter was anatomically correct, much to the amazement of the others, who persisted in wandering through it multiple times.

Museumed-out, Joan's family took cabs back to their hotel, and Joan and Jay began walking to her apartment.

"I don't want my mother staying in my apartment." Joan groaned. "We have to reassure her so she feels comfortable going back to Medford with the rest of the family."

"I'll talk to my cousin, and I am sure those two policemen will not make themselves scarce. They will be back for more questioning, if not today then tomorrow, and we can request police protection from them as well. We can talk to the other tenants in your building and make sure everybody locks the first-floor door to the stairway in addition to their own apartments. Everyone has gotten casual about that. Randy and I'll need keys. I'm sure he'll be happy to stay as well. That won't be a problem for him," Jay said, winking, trying to lighten the situation. "Let's walk to my apartment together so I can get some things for my stay. I don't want to leave you alone just yet."

"Thank you, but, oh boy, between you and my mother, I'm feeling stifled."

"It's just for a little while. This case is clearly coming together, but it's a risky time."

They arrived at his apartment, and he stuffed some clothes into a gym bag and grabbed his toiletry bag with his shaving gear and his toothbrush.

Joan sat waiting on the edge of his bed and then flopped back. Half sitting and half lying down, she felt like her own posture—in the middle and nowhere. She was exhausted. She was still in pathology. Tomorrow, she would be in the morgue, which she had to arrive at through the hated tunnel. She had thought her fear of it was over now that the snatcher was caught, but no, now there was a replacement snatcher who could lurk there as well. Her mother and Jay both wanted to stay with her—an impossible situation!

Jay exited from the bathroom, put his bags on the floor, and joined her on his bed. "Come on, sweetie. It's not so bad. Randy and I will join you and Kathy for a week or two. It'll be fine, and probably fun." He leaned over to kiss her.

She was not so welcoming to a kiss at that moment. He sat back and looked at her. She looked up and reached to pull him toward her.

"I'm sorry. I'm just feeling overwhelmed. Of course it will be nice to play house with you, and Randy and Kathy. I just want this thing to be over, and I thought it was."

"It will be, just not yet." They hugged and held each other.

"Do you think it would be better to stay somewhere other than my apartment, since they seem to know where that is?"

"Maybe, but there's not enough room in my apartment or Randy's, and we both have roommates. The four of us can stay comfortably at your place, and we often do already. I think we will be fine, especially if we can recruit a police presence."

Jay gathered up his bags, and they started back to her apartment. This evening, they were meeting her family for the final Chicago dinner. Their plane was leaving the next morning. Joan was formulating a response to her mother's offer to stay in Chicago, when they saw Randy and Kathy out running together. They waved them down, recounted the morning's events behind the museum, and presented the proposed plan.

"Sounds good to me," Randy said. "I can get my gear after Kathy and I finish our run and shower."

"On our way back to the apartment, we can get duplicates of my first-floor master key for Jay and Randy," Kathy said. "We're in."

"Thanks, guys."

With that, they went their separate ways.

On arriving, Joan and Jay knocked on Erin's door and were greeted by Erin's dog, Lily, shouting her hello bark.

"Hi, Lily," Joan said through the door. "It's just me, Joan." Before the barking could cease, Erin opened the door.

"Hi, guys. What's up?"

"A few things," Joan said. "Can we come in for a minute?"

"Sure. Want some iced tea?"

Both nodded as they sat on the navy blue velvety couch in the Erin's living room. When she returned with the iced tea, Joan, having sunk into the comfortable sofa, began reporting the morning's adventures at the pond behind the museum. She discussed their plan and urged the locking of all doors and general vigilance. Erin, familiar with the baby snatching events, needed no further background or urging.

"Jeeze! Sounds like this drama's continuing. I thought it was over, and now there's a new chapter on the home front. We'll have to watch out for each other and any strangers around the apartment building. I'll warn the Smith family on the first floor so they're up to speed, including that there may be a police presence. That would freak them out if they weren't updated. Oh, I meant to tell you Jackie was asking about you."

"How so?" Joan asked.

"Just pleasantries. She wanted to know if you were still on pathology, if I'd seen you recently, and how you were doing. You know, she's concerned about *her* medical students and patients. She also mentioned Shirley and her baby. Evidently, she had talked to them recently and they were fine."

Hmm. She wasn't so pleasant the last time I interacted with her. Joan decided not to comment on this. No reason to negatively impact Erin's view of Jackie.

Goodbyes were said, and Joan and Jay moved up the stairs to the tune of Rusty's barking.

At least we have watch dogs—two, Rusty and Lily. That's some comfort.

Upon arrival, she leashed Rusty, and the three of them headed back down the stairs.

"What do you think I should tell my mother?"

"You can update her on the plan and maybe promise to call her every night so she doesn't worry."

"Not bad. I hope it works."

Rusty did his jobs, and they had arrived back at the apartment building's outside door. Joan pulled out her key to open it, a good new habit.

They didn't notice a tall man wearing a fedora following their path with his binoculars from a block away.

TWENTY-THREE

NORTHERN MOCKINGBIRD: Mimus polyglottos

A slender gray bird with distinctive flashing white wing and tail patterns, known for vocal copying of other birds and even pieces of machinery, such as typewriters.

June 1980, Chicago, Illinois

JOAN WAS IN HER apartment to stay for a couple of hours—at last!

Jay, who had followed her through the door, reached around her shoulders and drew her to him. "This is all going to be fine. We have a plan. We just need to keep to it and follow along until the police solve this crime completely."

"Crimes. There is more than one—a murder and two kidnappings!"

"You're right, but the principle still holds, and one kidnapping is at least partially solved."

She turned around and looked up at him, which led to lips meeting with a warm, lasting kiss.

"I'm not going to let anything happen to you." He smiled down at her.

"I'm certainly not going to object to that, as long as it doesn't result in smothering me."

"You drive a tough bargain," he said as he gently pushed her away. "Let's get showers and prepare for the last supper."

They both eased into her bedroom and, after undressing, slipped into the shower together. It was a very, very long shower with a lot of activity in addition to bodies being washed. They ended up sitting on the shower floor, holding each other.

"My fingers are totally wrinkled!"

"This is a problem with a simple solution. We just have to get out of the shower." He grinned.

Joan was standing before her closet. *What shall I wear? I don't want to be too girly. A major goal for this evening is to convince my mother that I am grown and capable and can take care of myself. I could wear pants, but she prefers dresses, so if I have a dress that fits the bill, that would be better.*

She decided on a knit ensemble with a cream turtleneck encased in a beige wraparound sleeveless dress, and some tan platform sandals. *This is more professional, and the shoes have the added benefit of making me taller.*

"No, wait. I think a jacket would be better. A jacket exudes capability and confidence." *Maybe it's because it's characteristically a male piece of clothing?*

"I have a navy dress with a light cream jacket with navy piping." *Great! A decision.*

"I'll top this outfit with my long pearls and the matching earrings."

A few minutes later, she stood before Jay, who was buckling his belt.

"Okay. That's fantastic. Just the right mix of femininity and power, and you look great as always."

"I have to keep you. You are just so uplifting, especially when I most need it." She reached around his chest and gave him a long-lasting hug.

"I'm not going to object to that, *and* I have no restrictive covenants. Unlike you, I'm not worried about being smothered. As a matter of fact, it sounds pretty nice." He grinned.

She threw him a disdainful look and shoved his shoulder as they walked out the door.

They had decided on a steak house for the family dinner at the request of their visitors. The answer to their inquiry was, "Let's have steak again. It's Chicago, after all." When they arrived at the restaurant, the others were just being seated.

"Hi, Massachusetts contingent," Joan said to her family. "Ready to go home tomorrow?"

"We need a little discussion," her mother responded.

Here it comes. But Liz surprised Joan. She reported that the family had reviewed the situation and their conclusion was, with the police monitor set in place and the other accommodations that they had discussed—and if Joan would call her mother each night before going to bed—Liz would return to Massachusetts.

Jay smiled over at Joan. This was exactly what he had suggested to her. She, of course, was greatly relieved but didn't want to show it too much. This was a win, but it had a caveat, though it was one that she was happy to agree to.

After they ordered, Matt mentioned he hoped their dinner would be less exciting than the last one they had shared. They toasted to that, followed by a toast to Alex's interview, and one to the solution of the current crime, and one to the family being together. The atmosphere held this light note throughout dinner. Following dessert, goodbyes were said and interspersed with urges to be careful, and hugs were shared all around.

Joan and Jay drove south along Lake Shore Drive. "Well, that went well," Jay said. I'm glad your mother's comfortable with being at her home and not sleeping on your couch."

"Me too." Joan sighed. "We dodged a bullet there. Thanks for your idea about the nightly call. You were right on target, and your suggestion enabled me to think about it, so I felt comfortable as soon as she suggested it."

"Glad to know I'm good for something."

"You're good for a lot of things," she shot back.

"I'll just take that as a compliment and move on."

They were turning the corner to Joan's block when she noticed a man in running clothes viewing her apartment through binoculars.

"Jay, is that a police guard or someone else? Drive around the block," she said as she ducked beneath the window. She could see the lights on in her living room and assumed Kathy and Randy were there.

Jay pulled the car around the block and moved to the side of the road to scout for other people loitering. "I don't see anyone on this block, but why don't you stay down. Do you know where there is a phone booth nearby?"

"The Museum of Science and Industry has one in its outer lobby, which is unlocked and well-lit, and the police are always driving by monitoring it."

"Good idea!" When they arrived, Jay said, "You stay down. I'm going to call your police friends and Randy to let them all know about this guy. Be right back. You okay?"

"Fine. I'll be right here cowering in the damn car."

"Joan! Come on. It's you they are looking for. Please stay in the car."

She nodded from her crouched position as he ran up the imposing staircase to the museum.

Good grief! I can't wait till this is over.

When Jay returned, he said, "The police are coming, and Randy is going to turn off the light and look for the guy. I'll drive by your block again. If he is gone, I will pull up in front of the door and Randy will let you in. Go upstairs with Kathy. Warn the neighbors. I'll park the car, and Randy will wait inside the door to let me in."

There was no one on Joan's street as Jay drove to the front of her apartment, so the plan was carried out. Sitting in the living room in the dark, the two roommates commiserated while Kathy watched the street below from the edge of the curtain.

"Your mother went home?"

"She is flying out tomorrow. Of course, she didn't know about this. I didn't know about this!"

"Are you going to tell her?"

"Not now! I am not going to let these criminals interrupt my medical education and my life!"

"I understand, but we'd all like you to keep your life."

Joan shuddered. "Of course. I'm with you on that."

"What do they want with you anyway?"

"I guess they know that I identified Ricky, whom the police now have in custody, and that I saw the other guy with the same tattoo today behind the museum. My best guess. Who knows?"

There was a knock on the door. *Tap . . . tap-tap. Tap . . . tap-tap.*

"That's Randy," Kathy said, "but I'm going to double-check." She looked through the peephole.

"You guys have a secret knock?"

"It seemed like a good idea."

"You're right. It probably is."

The boys entered the apartment and assured the girls that all seemed quiet. Jay and Joan were very full after their steak dinner, but a little relaxation with a beer until the police arrived seemed like a good idea. The four of them sat, Jay and Joan on the couch and Randy and Kathy in the adjacent overstuffed chairs.

Jay leaned against Joan. "You okay?"

"I guess." She leaned back.

The police called from their car to be let in at the downstairs outer door. Jay went down to greet them, the three arrived at the inner door, and Jay used the knock. Joan opened the door, and the two familiar cops showed their badges per protocol.

"I thought we were done," Joan said, "but here you are. There's not much to say. We talked earlier today about the tattooed man behind the museum. That was pretty dramatic! Nothing has happened since except that about half an hour ago, coming home from dinner, we saw a man across the street with binoculars looking at our apartment. So these guys are still around, though we don't see them now."

"What did he look like?" the taller cop asked.

"He was in running clothes and had binoculars. That's all we saw. It was dark."

Randy and Kathy confirmed they couldn't see any more than that from the window but said as the man walked away, he may have had a limp.

"Which leg?" the policeman asked.

"The left."

"We're going to have a detail monitor the block. You have our number. We'll stay close. Be careful."

"I'm going to the hospital tomorrow," Joan said.

"Look out the window before you leave the apartment. Anything out of the ordinary, call us. We'll escort you if necessary. If not, walk with someone and go in daylight."

The four slouched in the living room, drinking their beers and trying to relax after their interview.

After sitting and just chilling, Jay said, "Randy and I will walk Rusty now. I don't want it to get any later."

Joan looked up. "I can't even walk my own dog?"

"Joanie, come on. Not tonight. Tomorrow, you and I will do it together."

"I guess I wasn't asking. I was just stating a fact."

"Let's not get maudlin. It's time to go to bed and get everyone tucked in for the night, including Rusty."

"I can't call my mom tonight and tell her that everything is fine."

"You just saw her a few hours ago. I don't think she expects you to call tonight."

Jay leashed Rusty, and he and Randy left the apartment.

"Kath, Jay is getting testy about this whole thing. I don't want my mom to stay in Chicago so I won't call her, but I am starting to lose it."

"A lot has been happening. I think we all need a good night's rest, and we'll be better able to think tomorrow. You're under a lot of pressure from all sides, and it is not surprising that you think you are losing it. Come here." Kathy walked over and hugged Joan. "It's gonna be all right. It's just not easy. We all love you, and we're going to get through this. Let's go to bed."

With that, the two girls went to their respective bedrooms.

Joan had a restless night, which meant Jay did as well, so there were two sleep-deprived people the next day. Kathy and Randy had left early, each needing to be in surgery. Joan and Jay rushed through their morning ritual, scanned the block through the living room window, and, seeing no one, were soon walking to the hospital.

Joan spied a mockingbird and pointed out its flicking tail and white lateral tail feathers as it flew away. "Sometimes I feel these perpetrators are mocking me."

"Don't spend any of your energy on them. They don't deserve it."

"Easier said than done."

"I'm sure you're right, but that doesn't mean it's not worth trying."

"I'm sorry. This is difficult for all of us. I just hope it's over with soon. Let's not let it get between us."

Jay nodded in assent.

While gathering her things from her locker, Joan turned to Jay and began to review the events at the hospital. "Okay, so what do we know? Ricky stole Denise's baby, who has not been found. It appears he killed Denise, from the evidence in her apartment."

"Yes, and next there was the tunnel."

"Right. I chased him in the tunnel when he took Shirley's baby, who was later found in his apartment and now is reunited with his mother. He was selling the babies, so the *why* is money—no surprise. The *who* is Ricky for the two kidnappings and the murder of Denise, but he isn't acting alone."

"We all saw another man behind the museum. You noted the same tattoo, and he clearly recognized you," Jay said.

"Right. Ricky was in police custody at the time, so there is at least one other *who* out there. Also, was the man watching our apartment the birder, or is there a third man? In addition, there remains the *how*. How are these desperate women, who might want to sell their babies, being identified and targeted by this ring of thieves?"

Jay smiled at her. "You'll figure it out, but you have to be careful. Gotta go. Lunch?"

"Sure."

She turned and took the stairs from the second floor in the main hospital up to the lecture hall. Today's lecture was on pathology of the skin.

TWENTY-FOUR

MOURNING DOVE: *Zenaida macroura*
Our most slender dove with a long pointed tail and black spots on the wings.
Doves pick food, seeds, and fruits from the ground while walking with mincing steps and a bobbing head.

June 1980, Chicago, Illinois

JOAN HAD LUNCH with Jay, and they walked home together when their work was done. It was about six o'clock, and the sun was still bright and its light comforting on this June evening in Chicago. Her family had left for home the day before, and Joan's life was getting back to normal, except for their extra precautions, which were not so very burdensome. After all, walking to and from the hospital together and living in the same apartment with someone you cared for could be classified as positives.

The outside door to her apartment building was locked, as it should be, and they used Jay's new key to open it just to make certain the duplicate worked. It did, and they could hear Rusty's greeting as soon as they began to mount the stairs. Smart dog! He clearly recognized their footsteps. His greeting bark was different from his alarm bark—lower pitched, less menacing. The whole setting was reassuring to Joan. Their precautions were in place.

Dinner finished, Joan pleaded exhaustion and moved toward her bedroom while Jay settled in the living room with this month's ophthalmology journals to catch up on his reading. Dressed for bed, she returned to the living room to share a warm kiss.

"I still don't understand *how* these women are being selected and targeted. There is something missing."

"Leave it for tomorrow. The police are working on it, and you'll think more clearly with some rest. A lot has been happening in just the last few days," Jay said. "Get some sleep. I'll be in soon."

Joan started to go to her bedroom but took an about-face and turned out the light in the living room. "Just for a moment. I want to check the street." She walked toward the window and peeked through the side of the curtain.

After watching for a while, the hair on the back of her neck started to stand up. "Jay, I didn't see anything at first, but then he moved."

Jay joined her at the window. As they watched, they noted a tall, barely visible man in dark clothing with binoculars directed straight at them. When Joan realized this, she gasped and jumped back from the window. Jay had moved to another window that was on the side of the room; it was not facing the street but had an oblique view of it. There he saw another figure with binoculars. He looked back at the first figure after Joan had moved from her viewing spot and noted the man's white teeth as he broke into a smile or maybe a sneer. Jay shook in anger as he realized the Peeping Tom had probably seen Joan at the window.

"Call the police! There are two of them, and I don't know what they are going to do!"

Joan quickly dashed to the phone and dialed 911, delivered the message, and then called the number of the two police with whom she had been working. "There's two of them. They are across the street with binoculars."

"We'll be right there. We are only about a mile away. Sit tight. Don't go outside!"

Joan hung up the phone.

"I think the second one is a woman. She has a shoulder bag that she just put the binoculars in. She must have some sixth sense. She is starting to walk away further up the block," Jay said.

"Maybe we should go down to the street to try to keep them around till the police get here," Joan said, moving toward the door.

"Are you crazy? We're staying right here as the police suggested. If they don't get caught tonight, it will happen later, but we are not going to put ourselves in harm's way."

"I really want them caught and gone from our lives."

"So do I, but let's let the police do their job," he said, moving toward her and hugging her close to him. "We should follow their orders in this case."

They watched together from Jay's vantage point as the man, who did have a slight limp, also disappeared from sight.

The police car pulled up, drove by, returned, and parked across the street. Before long, there was a familiar knock on their door. Someone must have left the outside door unlocked!

Good grief. Joan waited as Jay went to the door to let the police in.

She walked to the kitchen and returned with four Cokes. "We're getting to know each other too well," she joked but then turned serious. "I want this over!"

"You're not alone," the taller cop responded.

Both Joan and Jay reported what they had seen, which wasn't much. The new piece of information was that tonight there were two and one of them might have been a woman.

The police were about to get up when one of them commented that they had found a lab coat in Ricky's apartment marked with the hospital's logo.

"Either he stole it or he is friendly with a hospital employee," the shorter cop said. "So be careful when you are at the hospital. We're not trying to frighten you, but just keep a heads-up."

For the first time, they did not exit with a "stay in town" warning.

Joan noted this with relief but turned to Jay and said, "I'm going to lose it here. Now I have to be careful in the hospital even when I am not in the tunnel." She crumpled into Jay's arms and began to cry for the first time.

"Joanie, you're right. This is getting overwhelming. Maybe you should think about going to Medford with your mom for a few weeks."

Joan snapped into gear. "No, I am not going to let these aberrant people interfere with my medical school career. I will manage this!"

They tightened their grip on each other, and Rusty nuzzled to be part of the pack.

"Okay. Let's get some rest."

They both, along with Rusty, went down the stairs to make sure the outside door was locked.

Standing in the bathroom, both brushing their teeth, Joan turned to Jay. "He probably stole the lab coat to fit in and not be noticed."

Once they were in bed, Jay slipped out to peek through the living room windows to make sure there was no one spying on them.

The police had told them they would set up surveillance in a second-floor apartment across the street. There was no one on the street, and the surveillance apartment had a light on. They were monitoring.

When he returned to the bedroom, Joan's soft, even breathing confirmed she was asleep. It had been a trying day, a trying few days, especially for her. She was getting some much-needed rest.

He snuggled in next to her and soon fell asleep himself.

The new day came soon enough, and the two of them were walking to the hospital when Joan heard the cooing of a mourning dove.

She soon spotted it on a power line above and pointed it out to Jay. "I hope we have no cause for mourning today," she remarked ominously.

Jay responded with a look of disdain. "C'mon, Joan."

She looked at him and shrugged as they continued on their way.

Separating at their lockers with a plan to meet for lunch, Joan took the stairs down to the tunnel to head for the microscope lab. As she moved through the tunnel, someone entered ahead of her going in the same direction. They were far enough along that they did not appear to see her and proceeded through the tunnel. Joan slowed her pace so she did not catch up, and she noted that the man had a limp. Her palms began to sweat as she made this observation. It appeared his left leg was injured in some way. Committed to follow the path she knew would lead to the microscope lab, she continued slowly, her eyes locked on the figure ahead. She dashed up the stairway, paged Jay from the phone just outside the lab, and waited for him to call.

"Jay, I just saw a guy with a limping left leg in the tunnel."

"Okay. Let's think this through. There could be more than one person with a limp. I think you should go to the lab. There will be other people there. Do your assignment. I'll stop by the lab when I finish clinic, and we can walk to lunch together. We can report this to the police tonight."

"Do you really think that's best?"

"I do."

She proceeded into the student-filled laboratory, and after placing the normal skin slide on her microscope platform, she quickly became submerged in the image before her. She viewed the abnormal pathology slides as well, totally engrossed. Before she knew it, her assignment was completed, and Jay was entering the lab to walk with her to the cafeteria for lunch.

Erin bumped into them in the payment line. "Hi, guys. How are you?"

"Great!" Jay said. "We usually don't see you in the cafeteria."

"Yeah. I'm eating late today. I have been helping Jackie search for her lab coat and sent Julie for my early lunch."

"She lost her lab coat?" Joan said.

"I guess. We certainly didn't find it. I'd better go. I don't have my full lunch time, so I am taking this back to the nursery."

Joan turned to Jay. "The *how*."

"What?"

"I bet it was Jackie's lab coat that the police found in Ricky's apartment. You heard Erin before. Jackie *keeps track* of her patients. She called Shirley to check on things. By being chummy, she has a link into this group of vulnerable young women of meager means who may become pregnant and be willing to sell their babies."

"I don't know."

"Well, I do. I am going to call the police and suggest they question Jackie."

"How about if you wait until this evening? We can walk home together and call from your apartment."

"I might just swing by the nursery."

"What!"

"On my way back from the library, I'll just pop in on Erin and offer to walk Lily if we get home before her."

"Joanie, do you think that's a good idea?"

"I do . . . I'll page you when I finish my reading and see if you are ready to walk home."

She left the cafeteria and took the elevator down to the library. After a couple of hours, she decided she would take a break from her studies and visit Erin. She entered the nursery and saw Erin on the far side consoling a crying baby. While walking toward her, she saw Jackie through the glass in the nursing station.

Jackie was not wearing her lab coat which she, as head nurse, wore all the time.

Joan kept her back toward the nursing station while talking to Erin, trying to minimize possible repercussions to her from their visit.

"Hi there. If you're going to be late, I'm happy to walk Lily. I'll be out with Rusty anyway."

"That would be great! I am staying longer because one of my colleagues has developed a fever, so I'm going to cover for her."

Halfway across the nursery, Joan glanced at the nursing station and saw Jackie following her movement. She sped up and waved to Jackie, who did not wave back.

On their way home, the buildings were washed with the warm light of a June early evening in Chicago. Joan updated Jay on the nursery visit with Erin. He used his key on the outside door, and they gathered the two dogs for their walk. They hadn't seen anyone on the street on their way in but confirmed this from their third-floor apartment when they picked up Rusty. The two dogs were thrilled with their walk and with going together. Always better to have a doggie companion.

The four arrived back at the locked apartment house, to Joan's delight. She and Jay had just sat down in the living room when the police called from their car to let them know they were at the door. Jay ran down to let them in.

Joan had Cokes out for all when they arrived.

"So everyone's been safe?" the taller policeman asked.

Joan and Jay nodded.

Joan couldn't contain herself and burst out, "We think we know whose lab coat you found in Ricky's apartment!"

The two officers looked up with interest as Joan reported her observations about the nursery's head nurse, Jackie. The jangle of her ringing phone interrupted their discussion and carried a call from the surveillance across the street.

"Don't leave your apartment! We have two suspicious individuals on the block."

"The detectives are here," Joan responded as she handed the phone to the shorter of the pair.

"We'll be right down. Don't let them get away!"

Then he looked at Joan and Jay. "Don't go to the window. Don't turn off the light. You'll signal them. Stay put! We'll be back."

The door slammed, and there was the clatter of heavy feet running down the stairs.

Jay put his arm around Joan and pulled her in. There was a warm hug and a tender, soft kiss.

"Maybe this will be the end."

They just sat holding each other, and Joan reviewed the pertinent questions. "*Why?* Money, of course. *Where?* The hospital with its possible anonymity and its tunnel system. *Who?* The victims were poor and desperate women who were caught at the bottom of society. *How?* The perpetrators were facilitated by a trusted member of the nursing staff who maintained contact with previous victims and their associates and facilitated their being targeted."

There was a call from the police car. "We just arrested two peepers, Nurse Jackie and her husband. Evidently, Ricky, the perpetrator we have in custody, is his brother. They have matching tattoos."

TWENTY-FIVE

DARK-EYED JUNCO: *Junco hyemalis*

The largest of the juncos, which are cleanly marked sparrows with striking white outer tail feathers. Territorial conflict is uncommon.

June 1980, November 1980, Chicago, Illinois

JOAN SAT QUIETLY crying in the living room on the couch in a tight grasp with Jay.

"Thank God it is over!" she murmured.

"I know," he gently responded.

They sat just holding each other.

"What's next?"

"Dinner," he said.

She looked at him numbly, unable to respond.

At that point, Rusty began to utter his hello bark as Kathy and Randy came up the stairs.

"What's going on? Kathy asked with a concerned look.

Joan looked up as the two took seats in the overstuffed chairs opposite them.

Jay gave a summary of the evening's events.

"Wow! Jackie was the pivotal piece! Unbelievable! Why do you think that she did it?"

"She is married to creepy Ricky's brother!" Joan said.

"Poor choice!" Kathy said.

"Ya think?" Joan responded.

"Joanie," Kathy admonished.

"Well, the whole thing is astounding!"

"You're right. It is, but she's a registered nurse with a head nurse position. Why would she risk all that?"

"Why would she marry a creep like Ricky's brother?"

"Smart but no wisdom?"

"I guess."

"Let's talk over dinner. We brought steaks to grill!" Kathy said.

Kathy and Randy rose to action, moving outside to the grill while Joan and Jay followed behind to the kitchen. Mashed potatoes and peas with mushrooms were prepared inside while the warm, smoky aroma of the grill came drifting in through the open door to the balcony along with Kathy's voice. "We've got a bird on the railing."

Joan peeked out. "It's a dark-eyed junco. They stay around all winter to keep us company."

"Steak smells great!" Jay piped up as he reached behind Joan to give her a comforting hug.

"Sure does!"

Rusty began his hello bark joined by Lily, the higher pitched in the duo, who was still at their apartment following her walk.

"That must be Erin coming to pick up Lily," Joan said. "Hi, Erin. Come join us for dinner."

Erin smiled. "Smells great! I'm in."

The five sat in the living room, plates on their laps, eating heartily while the two dogs lay at their feet hoping for leftovers. After a few bites, Joan began to fill Erin in on the night's happenings.

"You have to be kidding!" Erin said. "Jackie, my boss, the head nurse! I can't imagine this is true."

"I understand, but sure enough, it is," Joan replied.

Erin went back to cutting her steak. "Well, I must say, if it weren't coming from you, I wouldn't believe it."

The conversation quieted down as all five concentrated on eating their delicious dinner before it cooled. Steak didn't come by very often and neither did warm, well-buttered mashed potatoes, for that matter.

"I'm speechless about this news of Jackie! I don't know what to say," Erin said. "She was a really good head nurse."

"Sometimes people make weird decisions that can have a major impact on the direction their lives take, and once they are rolling along, it's hard to turn back," Joan said.

"Poor Jackie certainly went on the wrong path!" Erin said as she got up to take Lily home. "Thanks for sharing your dinner. It was fantastic. I didn't get much for lunch today—busy nursery. I'm still stunned with the news." She waved as she moved toward the door. "'Night."

Five Months Later
November 1980, Chicago, Illinois

Thanksgiving was just a week away, and Joan and Jay were going to fly to Medford to share the holiday with her family. Tonight, however, they were having their own celebration dinner. Kathy was using her culinary talents on a small turkey, which was now in the oven. That taken care of, she was overseeing Joan preparing a pumpkin pie and the boys cutting up sweet potatoes for a casserole and broccoli for steaming. Kathy was whipping up hollandaise sauce for the broccoli and later would prepare the gravy. Erin arrived just in time for eating and was greeted by the combination of wonderful aromas of roasting turkey and pumpkin pie as she carried in her rich red cranberry sauce and green salad.

They were going to manage five people at the tiny wooden table in the kitchen, which was set, olives and all. They served on the counter, and everyone managed to get to their motley chairs and squeeze their plates on the table.

Jay raised his glass. "To giving thanks, great friends and 1980, a year of unusual happenings!"

"Cheers!" everyone echoed.

As they began dinner, Joan turned to Erin. "So how does it feel to be head nurse?"

"Daunting, but I'm thrilled to have the job!"

"You'll do fine," Joan replied. "I heard from Sarah last week. Anna is growing and hitting all her milestones. Sarah sounded very happy. She also said that she and her sister, Jill, were planning a dinner for their family and all were well."

"What about Jackie and Ricky and his brother?" Randy asked.

"My cousin tells me the trial will be coming up soon," Jay said.

Randy looked at Joan and Erin. "Do either of you have to testify?"

"Not sure."

"Me either. I hope not," Erin said. I still feel bad for Jackie. Sorry she went astray."

"But Denise died. She was murdered!"

"I know. My feelings are so mixed," Erin said.

"Well, I'm just glad it's over. The perpetrators were found. The baby ring is in the past. The trial is about to happen. I can close that book!" Joan declared.

"Hear! Hear!"

All raised their glasses again.

EPILOGUE

December 31, 1980, Chicago, Illinois

IT WAS NEW YEAR'S EVE, and Joan lay in bed musing. Jay was in the emergency room. An open globe had come in, and they were heading to the OR. It would be a late night. Joan was reviewing her day and her life and where it was going. What specialty? She should soon decide.

Peds, pediatric surgery, OB—these she had considered. Ophthalmology, which Jay was advocating. She should try to get some exposure. Public health—she had no experience, but her aunt Eleanor had introduced her to several milestones, as they occurred, a century ago. She felt she had participated in these giant leaps. John Snow and the cholera epidemic in London. Semmelweis and puerperal fever in Vienna. What was next in her life's plan? What specialty?

Of course, then there was Jay. They needed more time, but things were certainly going in the right direction.

And Aunt Eleanor? Would she be visiting again soon?

Well, everything isn't tied up in a neat little pink bow. But life never is until it reaches the end, and then it's probably a black bow, and I'm not ready for that. So bowless it is! And onward!

ACKNOWLEDGMENTS

This is my first novel, which simply means that I am greatly indebted to many. This book began during a Michigan State Coursera Course by David Wheeler. My fellow classmates, Ene George, Vicky Christodoulou, and Mieko vetted each of my chapters, as I did for them. Joan Stelmack and Joan von Leeson supported me in the table reads. Barbara McDonald, Nance Hoder, and Jane Kivlin all read my first draft, painstakingly, as I am sure it was. My developmental editor, Monti Shalosky, "held my hand." The Cadence group facilitated the publishing of this, my first novel. Thank you to all!

BIBLIOGRAPHY

Blackwell, Elizabeth. *Pioneer Work in Opening the Medical Profession to Women.* London and New York: Longmans, Green, and Co., 1895.

Ehrlich, Paul R., Dobkin, Davis S., and Wheye, Darryl. *The Birder's Handbook: A Field Guide to the Natural History of North American Birds.* New York: Simon and Schuster Inc, 1988.

Nimura, Janice P. *The Doctors Blackwell: How Two Pioneering Sisters Brought Medicine to Women and Women to Medicine.* New York: W. W. Norton & Company, 2021.

Peterson, Roger Tory. *A Field Guide to the Birds.* Boston: Houghton Mifflin Company, 1947.

Renehan, Edward J., Jr. *The Secret Six.* New York: Crown Publishers, 1995.

Sibley, David Allen. *The Sibley Guide to Birds.* New York, Alfred A. Knopf, 2000.

Wooded Island Birding Group as reported by Jennie Strable.

ABOUT THE AUTHOR

Retired pediatric ophthalmologist Marilyn Baird Mets, MD, has been administering medical and surgical care to the eyes of the children of Chicago for the past several decades, during which time she has been considered a Top Doctor by multiple national agencies. A professor at Northwestern's Feinberg School of Medicine, and the division head at Lurie Childrens' Hospital for twenty years, she has published over 110 peer-reviewed papers in the medical literature. She has served for eight years as a director of the American Board of Ophthalmology, the third woman since its inception in 1916, and as the fourth woman president in the 157-year history of the American Ophthalmological Society, and to date, the only woman president of the Costenbader Society. Since retiring, she has written her first novel, *Code Pink*.

www.ingramcontent.com/pod-product-compliance
Lightning Source LLC
LaVergne TN
LVHW091632070526
838199LV00044B/1031